Crickets...
And Then She Cried

Patricia Evans Dulin

Entegrity Choice Publishing
PO Box 453
Powder Springs, GA 30127
info@entegritypublishing.com
www.entegritypublishing.com
770.727.6517

Printed in the United States of America

Library of Congress Cataloging-in-Publication Data
ISBN 978-1-7351739-3-1
Library of Congress Control Number: 2020915382

Dedication

I dedicate this book to my husband, Shawn Maurice James-Dulin. You have been the rock I needed to follow through with this project. I thank you for supporting me in being transparent and open about what has taken place not just in my life but in our marriage as well. You are truly a man of God, an outstanding husband, phenomenal father, and an incredible human being. I can't fathom doing life with anyone else. I love you Dulin!

Acknowledgements

My children, you endured a lot but came out strong on the other side. Mommy loves you and knows that God wastes nothing so all that you have been through will be used for your purpose and for His Glory.

My sister, Dr. Gladys M. Peoples, thank you for pushing me in more ways than one. You challenge me daily, to not accept anything other than God's best for me.

"Mark, Luke, and John"—"the fact finder, the presenter, and the closer" you know who you are; thank you for continually encouraging me even when you do not know it. We have been down for each other like four flat tires for a few years now. Although we have known each other much longer than that, God is very strategic when it comes to who walks with you in your season.

Thank you, Brenda Major, the prayer warrior who specifically prayed for this project, also for helping me put my thoughts on paper.

Last of all, to the rest of my supporters, your constant unconditional love and prayers got me through some horrible experiences, and with you wanting to see me survive, I was able to make it to the other side.

Foreword

I applaud Patricia for her bravery and courage to go where a lot of people who never dare to tread…openness and honesty about her past and her pain. It doesn't end there however; it ends with the joy and hope that we don't have to stay stuck in our past or our pain. God wants us to come boldly into the throne room in our time of need to obtain mercy and find grace *(Hebrews 4:16)* and that's exactly what this book portrays. We can be free if we run to Jesus. You can be free too.

Pastor Hope Carpenter
Redemption Church

Contents

Introduction

When we hear the word *cricket* as it relates to the pesky insect, we instantly think of the noise it makes that keeps us up at night. When we take the same word, speak of it in a different context—relating to humans—we are confronted with silence when one expects words to be spoken. The sound of the cricket is loud and specific. This sound may be soothing at times to some and annoying at time to the same individuals. The "chirping" sound called *stridulating* seems to be most noticeable during silence.

The male cricket produces a sound near dusk during the mating season to attract female crickets and also to inform the other male crickets that the area has been spoken for. At that time of the day, we are typically eating dinner, watching television, or unwinding from the day. The sound is there, yet, because of our own "noise" we do not hear it. The second we shut everything down and lay our pretty little heads down to go to sleep, it's like a bullhorn has been attached to the cricket and it's all we can hear. The sound of a cricket can be heard almost fifty feet away. One of the cleverest aspects is, it's at such a unique frequency it's hard to pinpoint exactly where the sound originates. One could walk around in their house for hours trying to locate it.

At this point, you're probably wondering if this book is about my life or an obsession about crickets. I simply want you to understand the uniqueness of the sound. The purpose of the sound that we hear externally from the insect can resemble the sound we hear internally. In other words, the sound can be loud, annoying, and misleading. However, it is my belief that the internal message of the sound can be the call of recognition, revelation, and restoration.

It is my desire that this book speaks to the woman who lives her life like everything is grand. She does what is expected, serves others to a fault, always puts herself last, stays a busy as possible; all because every time she gets quiet, she experiences that internal sound. The sound that beckons her attention to recognize and acknowledge the "whys" behind the "whats." This can be a very tough stage as she visits the hidden scared places that knowingly or unknowingly emerge between joyful and rewarding memories and because she does not know how to reveal what she has been dealing with secretly for years.

This is for the woman who has recognized and acknowledged all the scares and struggles that are synonymous with that relentless sound. She is ready to reveal what has kept her hostage within herself and paralyzed her from reaching her full potential.

This is also for the woman who has found the courage to speak about her abuse, weaknesses, struggles, and brokenness. The woman who is fighting against persecution and judgement mainly from herself. She must believe that she is not what she did or what was done to her. At this point, the sound may return, causing her to experience familiar negative emotions. She must continue to see herself victoriously walking out of her wildness. She must keep her mind set toward good things. She cannot allow the internal chirping to take residence in her mind, causing her to focus on what happened versus the fact that God wants to restore all that was lost. Tragedies that occur in our lives can start out as such but with prayer, wise counsel, and obedience, what the enemy meant for evil, God can work it out for our good.

Regardless to which woman you identify with, whether it be yourself or someone close to you, or you just want to see how to get through the wilderness to find your God-given journey, this book will speak to you.

1
Beginning of the End
(So I Thought)

Those three semi-trucks right there. All carrying a full load. Looks like one of them is hauling livestock. Perfect. Impossible to avoid an accident; this accident; my accident. But, is it still an accident when it's intentional?

I'll just squeeze in between those two. They'll hit the other one trying to miss me. Those poor hogs. Ham and bacon for everyone! *That is horrible*, I thought, but still snickered. No way I'll survive this suicide attempt.

I must have replayed this scene in my head a dozen times since I received a devastating call from my husband. It was the perfect set up: two semi-trucks to my right and one behind me. All I had to do was position myself the right way. According to everything Daddy told me, the cabs would detach from their loads. Some may say I was being selfish, but on the contrary. I didn't actually count the other cars on the road or take into count how it would affect them. I just prayed that God would protect them.

Let's Rewind…

It began as a beautiful sunny day in June. Could it have been more perfect? I didn't see how. Actually, it could have been storming that day and I wouldn't have noticed. I was good, really good for the first time in a long time. Everything about my life was finally falling into place.

Job—check!

My boss—check! She was all around amazing. Really! Not many people can say that.

Kids—check! I have great kids. Talk about unconditional love!

Love life—double check…just not with my husband.

Aside from the birth of my three kids, this was the happiest I'd ever been. Yeah. Until the call…

I can still remember every word; probably because each one felt like a shard of glass, bursting my perfect bubble, then stabbing my heart. Still not free. Still not whole.

I was having a great day at work. Honestly, most of the day I was watching the clock, anticipating a great evening. I wondered what surprise would await me after work? Plans made that I didn't have to be involved in but knowing that my needs and desires would be considered and met. Would the evening start with "sit back and relax, I got you" or "get dressed, I'm taking you to this super cool place"? Whatever it was, I could not wait to blow this popsicle stand.

The phone rang, and the words "When were you going to tell me?" came from the familiar voice that used to give me comfort. This time, my husband sounded more like a stranger. Or was I the stranger in my house? No matter. And talk about cutting to the chase. One minute I'm floating on a cloud. The next I'm plummeting off a cliff with no parachute.

My husband…my loving—wait, how did he know? My mouth was moving, but no words—no words were coming. My heart stopped. My lungs collapsed. No air!

"You heard me. Answer my question," he barked.

Crickets… more crickets…then the tears.

Shock, anger, yep, anger came over me. There was so much swimming around in my head I couldn't form any words to fire back at him.

"Never mind," he snapped. "I'll get answers." He hung up on me. And that was that.

I tried to figure out what just happened. *Why is my sunshiny day drastically turning into a tsunami?* I sat there, in silence, until…

The phone rang again. "Really!" I screamed as I glared at the phone screen. I didn't even know my oldest brother's number was in my phone. I hadn't talked to him in years. And I wasn't about to now. I tried to pull it together, still hoping to salvage my evening…*our* evening.

"You're freaking kidding me!" My phone was blowing up again. What is this—tag-team brothers trying to take me down? Like I could get any lower now. Sorry, Jeff, not today. Why haven't you called in the past three years? I yelled, slamming my office door so hard that the wall shook. I was hot!

"Hi, Patti. How's everything going? I was just thinking about you," I mocked as the call went to voicemail. I waited for the beep, so I could hit delete. But of course while I was waiting, it rang again. I almost picked up the call, but by now I knew Shawn had probably sent a group text to my siblings, and God knows, who else—the pastor and First Lady? Probably.

I never turn off my phone, in case one of the kids call, but that's sure what I wanted to do. I collapsed into my chair, waited for my sister, Janice, to join everyone else in voicemail land. I stared at the screen then checked my watch. Bam! Sissy! This means the three sisters have talked and are now trying to determine whose call I'm going to answer. Well…I couldn't pick up and talk to Olivia now, could I? Everyone else would be even more upset because I didn't talk to them. Too bad! I could use some advice from her about now. What? No voicemail? I was on sibling overload when Elizabeth called. I was fuming. My head was throbbing and I wanted to curl up in a ball under my desk and disappear. I thought about that, but eventually I'd have to come out, or lie under there until I eventually expired and started to decompose. Would anybody even notice? I honestly didn't know. Not anymore.

"Let's just get it over with," I mumbled to myself, as I exited the building, trying to avoid talking to anyone. That wasn't hard to do, since just about everyone had already gone.

"Let's just end it all," I said, as I felt a pity party coming on. I was clutching my phone so hard I thought it was screaming when it rang and vibrated. "No, no, no!" I screamed in the practically empty parking lot heading to my car. My heart was pounding like I was in mile 20 of a marathon. My head was about to explode, but I had no choice.

"Hi, honey," I said, sounding so weak I didn't think my daughter would even recognize my voice. That didn't matter, since that's about all she allowed me to say.

"Are you happy now?" she screamed into the phone. "You just ruined my life. And for what? Daddy wasn't enough for you? Nothing is ever enough for you. You have to ruin everything and everyone. You know how important Coach is to me, to my career. Why? Don't even try to answer. I don't wanna hear anything you have to say. Just take a bow, Mom. Congratulations! You set me up and knocked me down, right down there with you. You win! I'm done! I don't care about those fake tears. I don't want to hear it. I don't wanna hear anything you have to say. I don't want to see you ever again. Do me a favor and disappear!" Then she hung up.

So much anger! So much pain in my daughter. She was right.

It was all my fault. I swore I would never make my daughter feel like my mother had made me feel. Unloved. Insignificant. But it had come full circle, hadn't it?

Through my tears I saw that I had missed a call. This time there was a voicemail. After seeing who it was and listening to the message, I realized he had called everyone. Oh God! I grabbed the side of my car to keep from falling to the ground. I glanced around, curious to see if anyone was around. Did anyone see me? There were a few cars, but otherwise the place was deserted.

"Nobody's coming to rescue you, Patti," I heard as if the voice was right next to me. "Nobody's coming. Nobody cares. You are nobody to everybody now." Chest heavy, I managed to climb in and start up the car.

"Go! Just go!" the voice in my gut was screaming. I was about to. But then—have you ever had that experience where you were talking on the phone, but don't remember calling or answering?

"Hello! Of course, I'm not all right," I heard myself say. "I should've figured he'd call you. He's been very busy ruining my life today."

"Patricia," my friend, Coach Mel said. "We'll talk it through together. You can't deal with this alone. You're not alone anymore. You're part of a team. Remember? Better united! I'll meet you at your apartment."

I wanted to. Needed to, I thought, but never uttered the words. Instead I just bawled.

"Patricia, I just hate this," Mel said. "It's not fair. You're such a strong, amazing woman: an incredibly courageous, beautiful woman. You want me to come and get you?"

"No!" I said loudly. I knew I was saying 'no' to something wonderful, life changing, even. I knew it way before then.

"Get in and drive," I heard very deliberately from my inner

self. So that's what I did. I didn't care where this voice was coming from. I was actually grateful not to have to think of what to do next. "It'll be quick, painless, and final. Everyone will be at peace, including you," the voice continued. "It's all in the timing."

As I saw trucks positioning perfectly to carry out my suicide attempt, suddenly, on my left, a white car appeared and slowed me down. I was frustrated. I blew my horn and peered into the window at the most beautiful angelic woman I had ever seen. Her flaming red hair was dancing around her flawless, caramel skin. Odd that her hair was blowing as if she was in a convertible since her windows were up. Even her blouse was blowing—no, more like swirling. She glanced my way and I quickly turned to focus on the road, then turned back to catch her staring at me—actually through me. I had this feeling I knew her, or that I had definitely seen her before. I could swear we had talked, but where? And why? And why was she here now? I felt this warm, calming sensation I'd never felt before. But maybe I had. How did I know her?

"So, this must be the angel of death or something," I decided. Was she there the first time I attempted suicide? Well, she needs to get it right this time. "Okay, go ahead and take me," I yelled.

But instead of her doing so, Mary (we'll call her) yelled back at me clearly saying, "You are stronger than this, Patricia. You are not alone. You are victorious."

"Yeah, right," I sarcastically replied. "And you are in my way, so move along lady, spirit, whatever you are. Girl, bye!" I shouted in disgust and embarrassment.

"It doesn't matter where you are," Mary said. "What matters is where you're going and what you'll do when you get there." Okay, first why am I talking to this 'woman'? And how can I even hear her? And what the hell is she talking about? Oh, and why won't she move out of my way?

I wanted to accelerate, but I was already too close to the car in front of me. The truck behind me wasn't close enough. This chick was thwarting my perfect plan. I threw my most frustrated look at her, like "Really!" She mimicked me. Then she smiled again and said "This is not the plan, Patricia. You will not die today."

I was about to give her the finger. I don't know why I glanced down like I was trying to remember which finger. Probably because I had no business doing it. When I looked back up, she was gone.

"Patricia, are you still there?" Mel shouted. I could hear the level of concern rising.

I quickly hung up. *How did I get here?!* To this place of complete confusion.

2
The Back Story

At this time in my life, we spent an abundance of hours in and out of gymnasiums for my daughter's basketball practices and games. We met hundreds of people and passed by twice as many. Life was so predictable and outside of a good game, it was mundane at best. Yet, this was all about to change as this particular day would turn out to be slightly different—to say the least.

I wouldn't call it love at first sight, but there was something I was feeling for sure. The thing that got me was her smile! That smile was like the sun bursting through the clouds, making everything—well, everything in my world anyway—look so bright and happy. It was a slow, easy smile, kind of like when it's been cloudy all day, and just when you think the day is spent, and somewhere behind those dreary clouds the sun is giving way to nightfall, it slowly appears, reveals its radiance, and says, "Hold on. Not so fast. Hi, there. It's me. I've been here the whole time, waiting for you to glance my way."

That's when I was like "hmmm," tilting my head slightly, like a flower to the sun. I think I might have actually exhaled for the first time. Humph! Amazing how the Devil doesn't present you with the apple until he knows you're ready to bite. Now that's a whole sermon by itself.

There she was, standing a distance away, talking with some adults who I'd seen before multiple times but hadn't met. She was smiling and laughing as if she didn't have a care in the world. Her laugh, although somewhat annoying had a cuteness to it that caught my attention; and that smile lit up the entire room. I took notice and filed it away as I had many others. Although I had seen her throughout the remaining basketball season, a year would pass before we actually connected.

My daughter was on an elite traveling team. And, not bragging (well, maybe a little), but she was one of the best players for her age. The lady with the sunshine smile was coaching another really good team. Ironically, my husband took note. He thought this could be a great opportunity for our daughter.

"Patient, supportive, mentoring, no wonder that team is so good. That's the coach that could take our daughter to the next level," he said.

I couldn't disagree, especially after watching how good the opposing team was and how much everyone was commenting about this coach. Someone said some kids had been given personal instruction and that was it for my husband. He nudged me to make the deal. It was like hiring a chocoholic to work at the candy store where Mr. Magoo was the manager. God help me. I prayed He would help keep my emotions in check and preserve my poker face.

I approached her, despite my spirit screaming "Run, fool! Ruuuuuuuuunnnnnnn!" That would be crazy, since no one knew the war raging inside me. "I can do this," I almost said audibly. With every step I asked God to assure me this would be okay. After all, Shawn and I were finally on the same page, studying to become licensed ministers. We were at the end of the course and man, was it good. We were learning so much about God, our relationship with Him, our relationship with one another, outside relationships, soul ties, etc. *This is a test.* Yes, that's exactly what it is. I am to put in action what I am learning in class. Maybe, somehow God wanted, no needed me to pass this test as some kind of purging or initiation. Maybe I was supposed to minister to her, to lead this already amazing person to a closer walk with me. I mean Him. Yeah. That had to be it, right? Riiiiight!

"Hi," I said. "My name is Patricia Dulin and my daughter plays basketball for the other Wildcat team."

"Hi, I know who you are," she said, "I'm Melanie but everyone calls me Coach Mel."

Honestly, I can't recall a single word after that. I walked away with a few dates, times, and a phone number so we must have said something. That assured me that I didn't just stand there like a deer in headlights. This will be a good thing for my superstar. My daughter would dub me Mother of the Year. And I was certainly being the dutiful wife, since, as I must remember, this was my husband's idea. But this giddy excitement I felt was so extra. Where is this coming from, and more importantly, where is this going?

I stayed through the first session because my daughter wanted me to and because no one leaves their 12-year-old alone with a stranger, even a great coach who they have no concerns about. I was also busy beating back my own, other feelings. And I was winning, convincing myself this was just admiration, nothing more. My daughter trained twice a week and by the second week she was very comfortable and so was I. I knew she would be fine with me just dropping her off. But I didn't…couldn't, any more than a moth can just fly away from the flame and not being afraid to be burned by the fire.

After a couple of months, Mel and I talked often by phone,

text, email, even that damn Facebook (the very thing that exposed it all). We talked a lot about my daughter, who the coach agreed could be phenomenal. We both loved basketball, so that opened the door and lowered the drawbridge (and both of our defenses).

I was always excited to share with her what Shawn and I had learned in ministry classes. We were diving into the scripture and discovering new things about the word of God to the point where I couldn't wait for the next class. It was in-depth bible study like I had never experienced. We attended four-hour classes, almost every Saturday for months, finished homework and exams as if we were getting a degree, and I absolutely loved it. I would discuss almost everything we learned with Mel and I thought I was helping to better understand some of life's daily challenges. She and I prayed together and talked about God and scripture; nothing different than I had done with other friends. I was doing kingdom work that led her to call me Minister Dulin when I was being "preachy." So, when my husband warned me about getting too close, I shrugged it off. "Please. I'm doing ministry," I replied.

Why did I feel this twinge of…I don't even know what… when we started talking about our relationships? I admired her smile even more when I learned about the load and misery behind it. See? I just need to offer a listening ear and a fresh perspective. It's all good, perfectly innocent. Right?

"Be more understanding. She's hurting, too," I remember saying to my husband. In my spiritual mind I was thinking: "Let's get everyone good and saved so we can all live right." In my arrogant flesh I was the relationship guru. Just call me "Iyanla, Fix My Life." I even suggested that me, my husband, Mel and her significant other go out sometime. Sweet baby Jesus! Where did *that* come from? Was it possible we could all be friends?

Who was I kidding? Shawn was already speaking of the warning signs.

I don't know what day it fell, my guard that is, but it certainly did. Mel and I had shared so much. I guess even the fixer needed someone to confide in. In my heart, I knew this was maybe the one person I could share what I'd been trying to hide, or forget or get past, practically my entire life. I think I was testing this friendship to see if it could hold me up, accept me and my past and really make the pain, rejection, and abuse disappear. I divulged things I hadn't told my husband and I was pretty sure I never would. I had an image to uphold regarding him.

Whew - Here we go, from the first time.

I phoned Mel and told her that I had something I wanted to share with her that I had never ever shared with anyone. "What is it? You know you can tell me anything," Mel said. "Hold on one second so I can turn off the TV. I want to be able to hear every word you say."

When she came back to the phone, I began to speak as if I was right back in that trailer being raped all over again.

I'm only seven. I cried. "I'm not a lady. I'm not a bad girl. I'm a good girl. I'm a good girl."

My cousin Jackson didn't listen. He just kept smiling and stroking me; first my hair.

"Ssssh. You have some pretty hair, Patti. And pretty eyes. It's okay. You can smile. I'm not gonna hurt you. We're just playing our new game. It'll be fun. You feel good, you know that?" he said rubbing my shoulders, before moving his hand down my back. "Real good. All plump and juicy," he said, squeezing my bottom. "See what you're doing to me?" he said, placing my hand on his thing. It felt like the dead snake my cousin Staci dared me to touch in the back yard that time. I took that dare. But then I threw it down and ran in the house to wash my hands. Now I was in the living room and when I touched it, it was hard and warm. I wanted to throw it down and run OUT of the house this time. It didn't really look like the snake though. I hadn't seen anything like it before, and I couldn't stop staring at it. He made me squeeze and rub it. He kept smiling and groaning.

"I should stop. This is hurting you, right?" I said, confused by the look of pleasure on his face.

"You can kiss it and make it feel better," he said.

"Un, uh. I don't kiss snakes," I said, pushing away.

He just laughed and pulled me closer to him. His hands moved fast, putting one over my mouth and the other was under my dress and in my panties before I—I wanted to scream. I wanted to bite him or something. But I knew if somebody heard me, I would get in trouble. So, I froze.

"Relax, pretty Patti," he whispered.

When he left, I remember trying to wash the blood out of my panties and off my favorite yellow dress. I scrubbed it and scrubbed it, then I scrubbed me. It burned, but I didn't care. I cried and scrubbed 'til I didn't feel anything. I just wanted to be clean but even then, I didn't think I would ever be able to wash hard enough to feel clean inside.

I was crying so hard; I didn't notice that Mel wasn't saying anything. But when I did, I started bawling. Dead silence on the other end of the phone made me feel even worse. But what did I expect? I was taking a huge chance. No longer was I Perfect Patti to her. This is one reason why I never told anyone about this. I had tried the day it happened, but…

"Just go to your room, then," I remember Momma saying. She was staring through me, but I couldn't decide if she was sad or mad. "You don't wanna talk, then I don't wanna hear it. You don't have a fever. Nobody wants to look at that pitiful face all day. Cryin' for no reason. Don't you have something to do?"

"Yes, ma'am," I said when I could feel my legs again. I wanted to say….I tried to…But, instead, I went straight to my room and grabbed my school bag. I don't know how long I was drawing and crying. When I was done, I was staring at a beautiful yellow flower with raindrops falling on it. I found my best shoe box under the bed and glued the picture to the lid. Then, still crying, I wrote a note to God and slipped it inside, before sliding the box back under the bed.

My thoughts and sobs were interrupted by Mel's gentle voice reaching through the phone and caressing me, apologizing, and encouraging me. So understanding and protective, I felt safe, understood, brave. Maybe, for the first time. I spilled it all— every encounter. By the time I shared about being raped by a pastor when I was sixteen, the voice was still encouraging, but there was anger, too.

Mel said, "That's so cliché, raping the babysitter while his wife was calling him from the other room. Where were your parents? Your siblings? Hell, did they at least tell the main pastor? No way this guy should've been allowed to "minister" to young girls or anybody for that matter."

My explanation only made matters worse. All those old feelings of brokenness, guilt, disbelief…unprotected; I suddenly realized the true meaning of unprotected sex. Nobody, not one person had ever protected me. My family knew about it but decided it was better for everyone to just never speak of it. *What's done is done.* "Better for everyone? What about what's best for me? Or was I nobody to them?" I asked out loud, as every bottled-up emotion came flooding through the phone.

"Where is he now? I want to get my hands on him," my angry protector fumed. "And everyone else who violated you, hurt and discarded you. Nobody deserves to be treated like that, especially not a defenseless child," she asserted.

Nobody had ever stood up for me like this; not even Shawn. But in his defense, I had never shared any of this with him. I was too ashamed. I would have to reveal that Perfect Patti wasn't really perfect.

The tables were turning, and I was being rescued now. Maybe we were saving each other from our past, from our troubled relationships. In Mel's relationships, she had so many obligations and responsibilities that those things became more important than the people in the relationship. There seemed to be no common interest between the two. They filled voids that were created from failed romances or just part of their personality, and she was content. No real love or passion either, at least not for the past couple of years. In my relationship, I was exactly where I NEEDED to be.

Listening, praying, counseling… it made me take stock in my own marriage. Yes, we were in ministry training, but I guess we skipped the chapter on ministering to each other at home. You know how you're listening to someone else's story, mostly the bad and ugly stuff, then you find yourself analyzing your own situation? The little cracks in my marriage seemed like gaping holes now. I don't know, maybe they were. Maybe I just needed a reason, no, an excuse.

3
Our Beginning

Like most relationships, it was good in the beginning. He was in college when we met. He worked as a trainer at the campus McDonald's, around the corner from my church. I grew up in church. We were at the church house so much I almost thought I was born in the baptismal pool. I can remember it like it was yesterday. You'll have to indulge me, because I love sharing this story.

I met my husband on a Thursday night after a church revival. It wasn't uncommon to head over to McDonald's after church. Maybe after the spirit gets fed the body says: "Hey! What about me?" Anyway, that night I was eating with momma, my sister, Pam, and my BFF, Crystal. Again, nothing unusual, except that cute guy who was really busy making sure everyone else was staying on task. I guess my sister was watching me watching him. Next thing I knew she got his attention and slipped him something. No way she would intercept…but I guess all's fair in love and war.

"Girl, I did that for you," Pam said, returning to her seat, noting the disappointment on my face. He glanced over in our direction and flashed a smile.

"You gave him her number, didn't you?" I asked, referring

to Crystal, still disappointed and a little ticked. I couldn't blame her, though. I had to assume he was looking at her anyway. Since everyone always did.

"My number? Un uh!" she said, a little too loudly.

"Butch would kill me. I mean he is cute, but y'all know Butch said God told him I was gonna be his wife. I am off the market. Whatever that means. Go undo that," she demanded.

"Would y'all calm down?! I gave him the number to call Patti."

"What? Me? Why?" I said trying to whisper.

"Cuz you're tracking him like a GPS. I told him you think he's cute," she said, crossing her arms like this was a done deal. "Give me some ketchup. My fries are getting cold."

"You had no right to do that," Momma said.

"You know that boy doesn't want no parts of Patti. If he did, he would've come over here and spoke without you meddling," she said before popping a Chicken McNugget in her mouth.

I was laughing on the inside at how she was eating. Normally I would smile at my own private joke, but I was mad at both of them, and embarrassed. And frustrated because she was right. He didn't want me.

"Now, Crystal," Momma said, "I know you wanna believe everything that boy says but you better be in prayer for yourself. If God didn't tell you what he told Butch, you might want to keep your options open," she said nodding in my future husband's direction.

I was fuming in silence. She was probably right about Crystal's situation, too. Suddenly, the double cheeseburger with no onion I had been craving for the past three hours didn't appeal to me at all. But I ate it anyway…in silence.

"Too bad," Momma continued, throwing salt in my open wound.

"If he did marry her, Patti wouldn't have to cook. That boy would bring home Big Macs and fries every night. He probably gets 'em free. That would make you happy, wouldn't it?" she said smiling at me. She was actually smiling!

"That wasn't funny, Momma," Pam chided.

"You all are just too sensitive. Your sister knows I'm just talking. Don't you, Patti?"

I just stared down at my plate of cold fries. I'm sure they were talking, but I was in my head, battling my feelings and I was losing—big time. The thing about my mother…well, one thing, is that she just didn't regard me. I mean she knew I existed, but she treated me more like a hearty plant than a person. One that you water whenever you think about it and it just seems to sit on a corner table not growing and not dying. Just existing.

Momma paid more attention to the kids she babysat than me. It sounds silly and selfish thinking about it now, but when I was a kid it really bothered me. Oh, who am I kidding? It *still* hurts.

There were always kids at our house. Even kids she wasn't paid to watch. Kids would just hang out at our house, especially in the summer. Can I just say I hated when relatives brought their teenagers to "hang out" at the house? I remember a female cousin who would visit in the summers. She wasn't much older than me, but she had way more worldly experience, even more than my older sisters. I dreaded the days she would get dropped off early in the morning. That meant I'd still be in bed and she would come and lay with me. In her sick game, I was Brian. She must've been in love with him, because she would get on top of me and ride me like a wild stallion. She bucked and then she would rub me like she was trying to start a campfire. All that moaning and groaning, and nobody ever seemed to hear it. Nobody said a word. Including me. This went on for three summers. But I was the plant in the corner. Plants don't talk.

I know you're probably wondering now why I love sharing this story. Here's why.

"Patti, look up," Pam said, kicking me under the table.

"Yeah. Earth to Patti. Where'd you go?" Crystal asked. She dug through her purse, probably not expecting me to answer. She pulled out a tube of lip gloss. Before I could even see the shade, she had applied it to my lips.

"There. Now look up and smile."

I did as she ordered, and I about had a stroke. He was approaching and smiling. He really was looking directly at me. Was I smiling? I hoped so. I was really trying to keep from fainting. I was sliding down in my seat when they grabbed my shoulders and scooted me up straight.

"Patti? I like your name," he said.

"I hope it's okay if I call, well, not right now I mean, I'm at work. And you're right here so, not near your phone. But I'll call you tonight," he said tripping over his words that were tumbling out. "I mean if that's okay with you," he said, looking at Momma now.

Momma choked on her drink and patted her chest before responding.

"Are you all right, ma'am?" he asked. "I can get you some napkins, or water. Or both, if you want. "

"I'm fine," Momma replied, sizing him up.

Momma said, "This soda is just a bit too strong, is all. It's getting late. We don't receive calls after nine on a weeknight. As a matter of fact, Patti isn't allowed to receive calls from boys."

"Momma," I groaned, my head in my hands.

"Maybe I'll make an exception but not tonight," she conceded, giving in to my look of embarrassment. Miracles really do still happen.

"I understand," he replied. "I'm Shawn Dulin," he said extending his hand to her. When she didn't reciprocate, he shook every willing hand at the table and held mine until I met his gaze. His smile was electrifying. Rockets were firing in me that I had never felt for a guy before. I couldn't help but to smile back at him.

"How about tomorrow at four then?" he asked, not taking his eyes off me.

Before I could get my brain in gear to tell my lips to move, Pam and Crystal replied, "Four o'clock will be fine." They giggled and I joined in and nodded at him.

"Four o'clock then," he confirmed. "I better get back to work and let you ladies enjoy your dinner," he said nodding before moving away to speak with one of the workers.

"He must be the boss," Crystal said.

"His badge said 'trainer,'" I said, proudly. And where did that come from? I didn't even know him. It didn't matter. He picked *me*. Shawn Dulin, McDonald's trainer, chose me. And he would call me tomorrow at four. "Ahhhhh!" I screamed with delight, in my head, of course. I dipped a fry in my pool of ketchup and wiggled it to my lips before snapping it up. I didn't even care that it was stone cold.

"It's just McDonald's. What's that—a dollar over minimum wage?" Momma said, shaking her head as she finished her sandwich. "And you really think he's gonna call Patti?"

"Yes!" we all replied.

"Humph!" Momma said, "Girl, don't get your hopes up. All the girls that come in here…he can have his pick. And I bet he does. Why would he want you?"

"I don't know, but he does." I blurted out what I thought was only in my head.

"He'd be crazy not to. And he doesn't look crazy to me. He looks kinda cute. Not *Butch* cute, but close," Crystal said, winking at me.

Well, he did call, exactly at four the next day. Just like he said. And the day after that, and the day after that, and…you get the idea. We had so much in common. He was easy to talk to. He actually listened and seemed interested in what I had to say. He had more faith in me and my dreams than I did. I asked him to come to church with me and he didn't hesitate. It was like he was waiting for me to ask. He told me he was raised in the church, by his grandparents. Shawn was always polite and respectful to my mother, regardless of her mood that day. My spirit told me he was a good man. He was fashioned (made) by God, just for me. If I had been waiting to exhale, now I could.

Okay, that was the best part. Oh, and I didn't want him to think I was playing any games with him. He had my number but I had never asked for his, so he was doing all the calling. Until one time I was talked into going to the drive thru at McDonald's. I was surprised to hear Shawn's voice asking for my order. I tried to be cool, but I was so nervous Crystal had to order or we woulda' got a bag full of nothing. He smiled so big when we drove around to pay and pick up our order.

"What are you doing working the drive-thru window?" I managed to squeak out in my nervousness.

"Waiting for you to drive up and make my night," he said, winking.

He can be so unapologetically corny and I still love that about him. Somehow, I managed to pay and grab the bag of who knows what. While we were grinning in a romantic trance,

Crystal grabbed the bag from me and pulled out the receipt.

"This isn't right," she said.

"What?" Shawn said, snapping back to the present. "I'm sorry. Let me take a look."

Since I was driving, she handed the receipt to me to give to him. I was still in 'la-la land,' so I had no clue what she was talking about. Shawn reached through the window and took the receipt, reviewing it.

"I put everything in the bag myself," he said. "What's missing?"

Crystal elbowed me and I just blurted out, "Your phone number. Uh, in case we get home and realize you didn't give us ketchup. I—we can call and—""And you can give us an extra order of fries next time we come," Crystal said, thinking fast, trying to rescue me.

"You didn't ask for ketchup, but I put some packets in anyway," Shawn said, still grinning and looking directly at me.

"Oh. Well that was very nice of you. I might just want to call to let you know I appreciate your great customer service," I said, proud of my quick thinking.

"You could just tell me that now," he responded, like a chess master putting me in check.

"Maybe I just want to call you to say good night and some other things," I said. It was my first attempt at flirting with him and that big Kool-Aid smile told me it was working.

"Other things. Like what?" he asked, his voice getting deeper and more sensual.

"Give me your number and you might find out," I said, growing more confident.

"Oh, I might?" he grinned.

"Only one way to find out," I replied.

Horns started honking and somebody was calling Shawn something over the drive-through squawk box that was definitely not on the menu. He whipped out his pen and scribbled down the number. He still managed to squeeze my hand for a second when he gave me back the receipt. I think I heard him say "I'll be waiting for that call," as we sped away, giggling.

Momma never apologized. Never said she was happy for me although she was extremely fond of Shawn. Shoot, I think she liked him more than me. I couldn't help but to think she was waiting for us to break up —holding out for her I-told-you-so moment. But it didn't come. At least not yet.

We dated for three years before getting engaged. Shawn took me ring shopping and I found one I liked—loved, actually. I wanted it right then. I know now how selfish I was, not even thinking that he might have something special planned. I actually threw a fit because they had to send the ring off to be sized. As I said, I wanted it now! I wanted everyone to see that not only did I have a boyfriend, but this man wanted me to be his wife. And the ring was proof of how much he loved me. I had never had anyone care for me as much as he did. But I was being such a horrible brat, Shawn confessed that he had my ring. Later that night we went for a ride and we went through the drive thru of the same McDonald's where we met. He ordered the same meal I ordered that night and then he proposed. Sounds corny, I know. But it was sweet.

Not long after the engagement, we were pregnant. This was planned, since we wanted kids right away. We were making quick marriage plans when we lost her. I was far enough along to know our baby girl, sweet Nicole. I was devastated. We both were. But I just couldn't show it. I thought I didn't really have a right to grieve—that this was my punishment for having sex out of wedlock. Unfortunately, people just assumed the miscarriage didn't bother me. That hurt. Looking back now, I wonder if Shawn thought that about me. No way! He was there for me through it all.

After marriage, we tried and tried, again and again. Shawn wanted so much to be the father he never had. I was diagnosed with endometriosis. Following surgery, I was told if I didn't conceive within thirty days, I would never have children. So, we kept trying. The only thing I conceived was bitterness toward every pregnant woman I saw, even family members. I wanted to give my husband what he wanted. And maybe I thought if I did something *normal* that would mean *I* was normal, whole, forgiven.

After a while, we came to the conclusion that maybe God wanted us to be parents to someone else's child. Okay then. If that's how it has to be. That's how it has to be. I had a family friend who knew a pregnant teenager looking for a couple to adopt her child. We met with her and planned for the adoption.

We were all in, very hands-on, attending doctor's appointments and basically took care of everything she needed. She lived with her mother who, by the way, did not want her to give the child up for adoption. But despite her mother's urgings, she said she wanted the best life for her child, and we could provide that. We had talked about our hopes for this child and already loved her like she was ours. The nursery was ready for our new addition. We were nesting.

Time passed quickly and soon it was the birth day. Shawn and I got the call to come to the hospital for the delivery. As I said, we were all in. When we got there, several doctors were present, preparing to turn our baby from breech position for normal delivery. Honestly, was there ever going to be anything normal in my life?!

They actually allowed Shawn to assist with turning his baby in the mother's womb. Not long afterwards, our beautiful baby girl was born. After getting assurance that everything was okay with her and the mother, we left the hospital to finalize things at our jobs for our maternity leave. I could recite Shawn's story by heart about how he helped to deliver our child. He must have shared it with a dozen people that day. He was beaming and I was so happy for him, I mean us. But why didn't I seem as over the moon as he was? I was waiting, as usual, for the other shoe to drop. It didn't take long. And when it did, it was more like a steel beam.

When we arrived back to the hospital that evening, a security guard and social worker stopped us at the door. It's never a good sign when they want to walk you down the hall to sit and talk. The social worker explained that the girl's mother begged, probably forced her to look at the baby.

"I couldn't intervene," the woman explained, "though I wanted to. She laid it on thick. She actually asked her daughter how she could give away such a precious gift to strangers. 'Not our blood,' she said."

"But!" I shrieked as Shawn patted my hand.

"Let her finish," he said, trying to console me as the tears welled up in his eyes as well as mine.

"She's a piece of work," the social worker continued.

"She asked her own young daughter how she would explain to this baby why she gave her away. She cried and laid it on thick. I can't tell you how many times I've heard grandmothers say something crazy like, 'How could you do this to me?' When she said it, I just shook my head and left the room. When I came back the girl was crying and trying to nurse. I'm so sorry."

"Just like that? She can't do that. We had everything all arranged!" I wailed.

"Those first 72 hours can be torture. No matter what arrangements you made, she still has three days to decide. It usually takes about 48 hours for the baby-daddy or, in this case, the grandmother, to convince mom to keep the child. This granny is so good, she only needed a few minutes. She promised her everything but a pony if she would keep this child."

"But she can still change her mind again, right?" I asked hoping for the last-minute miracle.

The social worker replied, "She can. But she'll be discharged tomorrow. And it looks like granny is hunkering down in that room for the night. If they leave without signing over her rights, that's it."

"Just like that?" Shawn asked, holding out his hands as if he was about to tell his delivery story again.

"I'm afraid so," she said.

So once again we left the hospital empty. I remember staying up late, writing to God again. I prayed, I drew, and I wrote and emptied everything inside me into my box with the yellow flower. I still kept it under the bed, like when I was a kid. Funny, I never took anything out to read it. I guess I was afraid that would mean God wouldn't respond. I just know I felt better after I deposited my note and shoved the box back under the bed. More hurt, more pain, more disappointment. Oh well, life moves on.

4
He and Me

In the midst of the current devastation, I wanted to tell my husband everything about my past, but I was afraid that it would drive him away. After a while, it didn't seem to matter. I decided since he loved me, I would love him right back the best I knew how. And that went well, without my having to open that box of pain for him to inspect. Maybe this would somehow redeem me. God would use Shawn to make me whole. But, as always, that was not to be the case.

No matter how much I tried in the beginning, my mind continued to drag me back. Not that I put up much of a struggle.

My past was filled with pain. As a teenager, I recall going to a family party with my aunt and two cousins. There were lots of other relatives there, so maybe that's why I got permission to go. I just wanted to have a good time. Dancing, eating and **do** what everybody used to talk about at school on Monday. This was gonna be my big party story. I couldn't wait.

He was twenty, tall, and cute with the prettiest hazel eyes. I think I was staring into them at one point, hoping to get a closer look. I watched him for a while, not caring if anyone noticed; and truth is, they probably didn't. He was so polite and soft-spoken.

He was being very attentive and helpful to the older folks. "How nice," I thought. "But, he's your cousin," I reminded myself. Not really, but our families were so close we were like cousins.

"Here, taste this," my aunt interrupted. "You'll like it. It'll loosen you up," she said, dancing around me. "It's a party, right? Have some fun, Patti."

I took a sip. It was sweet and smooth. I coughed.

"You have to drink it slow," she coached. "This is grown folks Kool-Aid. You're growing up, girl. Starting to look like a grown woman."

I took a slow sip. Then another, and one more.

"All right, that's enough," she said. "Just be sure you eat something and dance off that buzz," she instructed.

We danced. First me and my aunt and then me and some cousins. I think he was watching but he never approached, at least not yet. Right at that very moment, "Oh God, no way, not now…I'm about to pee on myself," I said to myself. I hurried upstairs, not bothering to lock the door, since everyone else was downstairs. Big mistake.

He just came right in. If he knocked, I didn't hear him. He must've followed me up here. I guess he had to go, too. He stumbled through the door, speech slurred and smelling like a fifth of moonshine. He told me to pull my pants down. Then he just pulled out his little man and told me he had to drain the venom from his snake first. I froze, like a mouse realizing it was about to be dinner. This is not at all the story I wanted to tell. No, I was sure I wouldn't tell this to a soul. He shook the "snake" and turned toward me. I wanted to scream, but what was the point. The music was so loud no one would hear me. Everyone was talking, laughing, dancing, and having a good time. Who cared what was happening upstairs? Surely somebody downstairs would need to come upstairs to the bathroom eventually. But I guess not. No one came to my rescue.

"Don'tcha think you should pull your pants down?" was all he said.

He didn't say anything pleasant such as, "You look nice tonight," or "I really like the way you dance."

Nope. *Pull your pants down* was all my obviously drunk, play cousin said. I was a little buzzed myself, but well aware of what was taking place. Mostly I was scared, mad, and disappointed. None of those emotions were compelling me to pull my pants down, though. I just needed to escape. His drunk butt was not backing down but I was pissed now. I pushed him back, darted out the door and ran down the steps and out the front door.

Once outside I caught my breath and collected my thoughts. One of the cousins I came with ran out behind me. She asked what was wrong. Fighting through all those emotions, I really did try to tell her, but she cut me off and said, "Girl, quit lyin. He wouldn't do that. You're just drunk." I think she believed that, or wanted to. He had everybody charmed.

Clearly, I wasn't drunk, but my parents would kill me if they knew I had been at that type of party let alone sipped alcohol. My father, being a recovering alcoholic, would have snapped me in half. I by no means wanted to disappoint him in the least, so, I kept quiet. No one would believe me anyway. And that story would never be told, at least not until I opened up my heart to Mel.

Growing up, I was sure I had a sign down there that read, "Always Open." I had seen those signs in the stores downtown, including my favorite place, Weaver's. My cousins and I would go there all the time for chilidogs, fries, and a coke. I remember one night, right before we moved from the small, one-stop-light-flashing-at-9:00-pm type of town to the bright lights, tall buildings, busy city; I had been packing all day. When they came by to rescue me for our "last supper," as we called it, I was almost too tired to go. That's a lie. I was tired, but nothing would keep me from sharing my favorite meal with my favorite girls, one last time.

We danced, sang, and laughed the whole way there, to keep from thinking about me leaving. It was the summer before my senior year. We couldn't wait one more year! Part of me was ready to go, leave my painful past in the past and get a fresh start in a big city. My older sister, Pam, was there and I was looking forward to hanging out with her, getting a job, maybe even a car, after I got my license. But tonight was just about me, and my two cousins who were more like sisters to me. Oh, and the best chilidogs and fries in the state of Kentucky. But, when we got there, we saw that sign. Not "Always Open," but the flip side, "Sorry, we're closed." We were all so disappointed. I just wanted to break in and grab that sign and put it on. But I wouldn't be sorry, just closed.

I wanted to tell my girls how my mother was working me like a Hebrew slave all day. "Wrap this again. Use more newspaper. These things are fragile, you know. We can't afford to replace the stuff you break being careless." Wow! Did she really care about these cheap plates and glasses more than me? Didn't she see I was fragile, too? Another tale better left untold. We ordered pizza and still had a good, though bittersweet, night.

I thought that would be the last time we were all together, but I'm glad I was wrong. A few weeks later, they came to Lexington for my birthday. They bought me a cool outfit and we were all matching, like TLC or somebody. It was so much fun, even Momma couldn't ruin my day with her comments that I should be in the background on the pictures since I was the biggest. I was sixteen and ready to make my own money.

I was on my way. Well…baby steps. Momma let me get a job babysitting. She thought if I had a real job, even part-time, I would neglect my schoolwork. She might've been right about that. I needed money for college, an apartment, a car, clothes, and other stuff. I don't know why people don't understand babysitters should be paid more the worse your kids are. We need compensation for mental stress, exercising restraint, and for not flushing your little demons down the toilet. But I digress.

You know what they say about preachers' kids (PKs)? They are the worst. I was expecting big bucks when my mother said our youth pastor and his wife wanted to hire me. But, as we know, nothing seems to go as I expect.

The kids weren't that bad, but they still wore me out. And their parents were late coming home. I remember lying across the bed in the guest room, thinking I would just spring up when I heard them come in. But what woke me was the jolt from his fingers inside me. I was horrified and confused. Why didn't I jump up and push him off me? Why didn't I scream? Afraid to wake the kids, maybe? What would his wife think? Would he tell her I seduced him? And why did I care? Scream! Scream for God's sake! While I lay frozen, he leaned down to kiss me. When his wife called out to him, he got up, sucked his finger, and then put it to his lips telling me to 'shush.' Which of course, I did.

The next time I wasn't so lucky. I was in the garage. I was looking for washing powder and disinfectant. One of the kids had puked on himself and on the bathroom floor. I felt his breath on my neck and his hand on my shoulder and I froze. Approaching me from behind, he put his other hand down the front of my shorts and his fingers found their spot again. Before I could protest, he had me pressed against the car, my shorts and panties dropped to my ankles and his penis was in me.

I remember thinking: "Is this better or worse than cleaning up puke?" Both were pretty revolting. He must've been reading my mind. He thrust in harder. I prayed he wouldn't cum in me since I was pretty sure he wasn't wearing a condom. Oh my God! Please, God! Don't let this man make me pregnant. Again, he must've heard my thoughts. He pulled out and ejaculated on the floor. Then as quickly as he had entered, he straightened up, kissed me on the shoulder and walked out. I pulled up my shorts and asked his wife to take me home.

On the way home, I couldn't help but think "What is wrong with me? What am I doing to cause this to happen again, again and again?" Whatever it was had followed me to Lexington and set up camp. I could've and probably should've kept this all to myself. Momma would kill me for causing a scandal in our new church and, as always, she'd say it was my fault for being fast.

"Always up in somebody's face." Her words slapped me so hard I think they could draw blood. There was no point in trying to defend myself to her. She thought I was the rebirth of Jezebel. I would have to tell her why I couldn't babysit any more. And, as much as I loved church, how could I go every Sunday and look at him, looking at me like I was his happy meal? Did his wife know? Was I the only one? How many other silenced victims were sitting right on those pews next to mothers who thought they were dirty temptresses? This time I couldn't keep quiet.

"You have to tell this to Reverend," Pam said after I spilled my guts to her. "He has to sit him down. Kick him out. Heck, lock him up for that matter; before Daddy kills him."

"You're right," I agreed reluctantly. "But maybe you should

tell him. I don't think I can say it again."

"I know it feels like you're reliving this horrible mess, but you only have to tell it one more time. Like you said, you could be helping other victims. Besides, we'll all be there for you," she smiled reassuringly. She grabbed me up in a big bear hug that I didn't want to end.

Sitting in the Reverend's office with Pam, Theola, and Elizabeth (three of my four sisters) felt surreal. After he led us in a prayer he said, "Now, tell me exactly what you think happened, young lady. Whatever you can recall." He cleared his throat, then took a big sip of water. "You sure I can't get you young ladies something to drink? Water? Water, anyone?"

What I think *happened? What I can recall? Does he think I'm making this up?* I thought. "Yeah, give me some water," I wanted to say. "So, I can throw it in your face and break the glass over your head. "

My no-nonsense sister, Theola, must've heard my thoughts. She squeezed my hand real tight and was about to speak when Pam jumped in.

"No, thank you. We don't need any water. Patti can tell you exactly what happened. She can recall it precisely, since it was so recent. Go ahead, Patti," she encouraged, smiling at me.

I know I was red as a beet. My face was burning, head throbbing, and I really just wanted to puke. This would be almost as painful and embarrassing as the actual encounters. Why didn't I scream right when it was happening? Why didn't I fight him and run to tell his wife? I knew my screams would be muffled in humiliation and guilt. Why did this keep happening to me? Was I causing this? What was I doing and how could I shut it off?

"Young lady, I'm waiting," yelled the Reverend. "Now, you

said this was urgent, so I adjusted my schedule to accommodate you," he said, disturbed by my silence. I was trying to get my thoughts together, but all I could hear was Theola, who I knew couldn't behave for too long.

"She came here to confide in you and she will. And we do appreciate you accommodating us, Reverend," she said sarcastically.

I began recounting every detail. I wasn't even sure he could hear me over the voice that I thought was coming from a corner of the room. I dared not look, but I could hear my accuser loud and clear: "He doesn't believe you. None of them do. Just look at them. Heads all looking down at the floor. What's down there, Patti? Ha-ha! It's your face, cracked and on the floor. It's your lies and cries for sympathy. Cry, Patti. That's right. You're always the victim. It's always somebody else's fault. Right?"

"You are in Christ," I heard a soothing voice say. "There is no condemnation for you. You are perfect. Whole. Nothing missing. Nothing broken. You are His righteousness," she said, smiling sweetly. "Now speak up."

I did just what the voice said, I spoke up. And as I spoke my confidence grew. My sisters were looking from me, reassuringly, to the Reverend. Honestly, I couldn't say what their looks to him were conveying. Everyone had a blank poker face directed at him, but I had a pretty good idea what they were thinking. I just kept talking, determined to get it all out. He wanted details and that's what I gave him. When I was done, I was drained. I really wanted that water but he didn't offer again. He didn't look at me either. He picked up his phone.

"Yes. Send him in now. Thank you," he said, then, hung up the phone.

For what seemed like forever, no one spoke. Theola squeezed

my hand again and Pam put her arm around me for a quick hug. Elizabeth mouthed, "good job," and gave me a thumbs up. I felt relief until the door opened and he strolled in. The Reverend gestured for him to take the chair that was next to him, behind his huge desk.

"This young lady has just told me about some indiscretions between the two of you," he said.

"She is our babysitter, that's all," The youth pastor countered quickly. "There were no indiscretions. I told her that when she approached me inappropriately. I didn't say anything because I thought she understood her place. Now what is she saying?"

"The truth, you—" Theola began.

"Now, I don't want to have to ask you to leave, but I will if I hear another outburst," the Reverend interrupted, scolding Theola.

"Now go ahead, young lady. Tell him what you just told me. The accused has the right to know. And please be succinct. I'm sure we all have other things to do today."

Was he kidding! Why should I have to go through this again? If he had something more important to do then maybe he should just go. But those pleading sister-eyes were boring into me, leaving me no choice.

I repeated every word, like I was reading a script. I coughed a couple of times because I was parched. But I refused to cry. I refused to look down. I stared into his eyes until the pervert started smiling. He even licked his lips like he was reliving the moments or thinking about the next time. Even though he was sitting behind that desk, I swear he was getting a hard-on, right next to the Reverend. When I concluded AGAIN, the Reverend asked if the accused had anything to say. He clapped. The prick sat there and clapped.

Looking directly at me, this jackass says, "Are you sure your boyfriend didn't do this"?

WHAT?! I said in my head. "Oh yes," I replied. "It was him." Everyone looked at me in shock, so I had to tell them I wasn't serious. The Reverend said, "This is not a joking matter, young lady."

"Ladies, I am so sorry you had to go to all this trouble to be here and witness your sister's tall tale," my accuser said pompously. "As I said, she's our babysitter. Or she was. Maybe I should have fired her the first time she came on to me."

"First time, you nasty, vile son of a—" Theola said.

"Enough!" the Reverend roared back.

"I knew she needed the job. And, Reverend, you know we've talked about these fast young girls coming on to me. This is just another one. As I said, I didn't want to make a big deal out of it and embarrass her. Actually, it was my wife who told me to just pray for her and let her go," he lied. "But I knew Christ would want me to try to help her, if I could. I thought if she saw what a loving relationship me and my wife have, she would realize she was out of order. When the time is right, your Boaz will come along," he said winking at me. "Until then, maybe you should fast and pray with your sisters to cast out those impure thoughts."

"That's an excellent idea," the Reverend said, sensing the righteous indignation rising in me and my sisters. "You ladies fast and pray. And, as we know God's love hides a multitude of sins, I think it's best we let Him work this out. We will trust Him and I trust that the six people in this room will leave here and not speak another word of this. Are we in agreement?"

I wanted to puke—and then punch them both below the belt, but of course I couldn't. None of us could speak. The Reverend excused the pastor and strongly suggested we not say anything to our parents. My dad would kill the perpetrator and end up in jail and as for my mother, she would have a heart attack and die. He asked if we understood and so we just nodded and left. We never spoke of it again. That vile youth pastor gave the message the following Sunday—about forgiveness!

Yes, I went to church after all that. I had loved church my whole life. It wasn't just a place to go. I felt like I was born in church and I was just supposed to be there. I loved everything about the Baptist church: the hymns, the service, Wednesday night Bible study, taking the Lord's Supper, and those special Sunday dinners after church, when the entire church family would eat together. I even went to business meetings with my mom when I was a kid. I didn't mind. I liked being there. I felt safe and important.

Sometimes, when I'm in a dark place, I remember those early church days. Like when we would go to fellowship with another church. The bus driver used to let me sit up front on the stool that separated him from the passengers. It was probably not safe, no seatbelts or anything. But I'm still alive. We would sing all the way there and back. Good times!

"Jesus loves me. This I know," I sang. Not long after I directed my first song in the children's choir, the choir director, who was also the First Lady, let me sing with the adults. This was way before I met the age requirement.

Oh, and those fashion shows. I can still see myself strutting in that red dress with the big bow in the back and that cute white hat and my white gloves. I begged Momma to buy me those shiny red shoes with the white bow.

"They're not practical, Patti. You'll mess up those shoes before I finish paying for them," she said. "Wear your black Sunday shoes. You'll be fine. You should be worrying about being a good girl for Jesus instead of always trying to get people to look at you anyway."

I don't know what Momma was thinking when she saw me hit that runway. Well—the middle aisle down the center of the church. But it was decorated like a runway. And I felt like a beautiful model princess. And everybody was looking at me. You could hear the *clack, clack, clack* as my new shiny red shoes hit the floor. The First Lady bought them for me. She was beaming and everyone was clapping—even Momma.

But that night I heard Momma and Aunt D talking. Momma said, "I told that child 'no.' And what does she do? Goes right to the First Lady and made her buy those shoes that she doesn't need and doesn't deserve," she said, much louder than she intended.

"Now you know Patti didn't make her buy 'em," Aunt D said. "I'm sure she just wanted to do something nice for her. What's wrong with that?"

"What's wrong is that Patti can be very manipulative. She has a way of getting what she wants," my mother said. "Lord knows, I've been trying to pray that spirit of manipulation off of her. I don't know where she got that. Must be from her daddy's side of the family."

"Are you sure about that?" my father's younger sister retorted.

I didn't know what manipulation was back then. I remember asking my sister what a spirit of manipulation was and she told me to stop listening to grown folks' conversations. When I asked her if we could still be sisters if the First Lady was my real mother, she told me to stop tripping. She made me swear to never say that again, especially not to Momma. I never said it, but I prayed a lot. I wanted God to answer that prayer so bad. So much that I must've cried for a week when she and our pastor moved away.

I told Momma I was crying because I had a stomachache.

She made me drink so much Pepto Bismol I knew I was pink on the inside. I couldn't tell her how much I wanted to run away and find my real mother. I tried to stay out of her way. I was in my room a lot crying, praying, drawing, and storing it all in my yellow flower box.

I wasn't playing about finding my real mother. I had heard so many stories, rumors that she wasn't my real mother. Not your typical, "go away, your adopted" kind of stories from older siblings when you get on their nerves… but real stories.

It all kind of made sense though. I was the youngest of eight children where seven were pretty much one to two years apart. Then came me, six years after the youngest was born. I also never really felt like her daughter. I felt more like—I don't know—a distant relative who had worn out their welcome. I picked that up from the many times she would just stare at me. "What!" I wanted to say. "Why are you looking at me like that? Tell me!" But of course I couldn't say it.

Thinking back, it never seemed like she enjoyed being a mother. It wasn't until I was in my wilderness that I understood why.

"Lord, please let me be the kind of mother to my kids that I wish I had." Well, that opportunity would take forever to come.

5
Mother, May I

Motherhood took its sweet little time coming. After a mis carriage, a failed adoption and numerous godchildren; it took six years and a miracle for me to become a mother.

As much as I loved all things church, I had never been to a tent service. A busy body from our new church told Shawn it was a healing service and urged us to go. "What do we have to lose?" Shawn said. "I'd say we're due for a miracle." He was right about that. We had lost so much already. We were due—no, over-due for a blessing.

It was a really hot night. I don't remember anything that hap-pened before an elder called me up for prayer. One of the church mothers, a sho' nuff prayer warrior, stood behind me. I placed my hands on my stomach. I believed and received every word of that prayer. I really felt different. Leaving there, I truly believed I would get pregnant soon. That's exactly what happened. A month later I was pregnant with our first blessing.

Because of the previously miscarriage and endometriosis, my doctor listed me as high risk. I didn't think about miscarrying this time. But boy was I sick. I puked through the entire preg-nancy, even while pushing her out. I mean who loses 30 pounds while they're pregnant? This girl.

When our first princess was born, the world could've ended and I wouldn't have noticed. Havilyn Faith Dulin (Have-a-little-faith) was the cutest little underweight baby I'd ever seen. Ha! I remember Shawn's shoe was bigger than her. She wasn't a preemie, just tiny.

Shawn was in love with her. No really. I felt like I had to ask for permission to hold her because he always had her. I get it. He was determined to be the father he had never had. My husband was happy and whole. But I wasn't. No time to analyze my issues because I was trying to keep up with our little firecracker. Walking, actually running at 6 and ½ months. Speaking in complete sentences at one and by two she was potty trained and dressing herself. Whoever said the first one gets out of the way for the next was not lying. Before her first birthday I was pregnant again.

I knew the gender of our first child, but Shawn didn't. I guess this would be our thing. He knew our second child's gender, but I didn't. This time I wanted to be surprised, but he didn't. I named him Shawn Evan. He was pale as paper with eyes as blue as the Pacific Ocean. Evan was a quiet baby. He didn't seem to require much attention. Everyone wanted to keep him because he was so content. Wish I was. The stress of having two babies, only sixteen months apart, then losing my job due to a closure, starting a new one, Shawn traveling a lot for work, and my decision to be super active at church…you get where this is going.

Our kids were the center of Shawn's world. I didn't want to burst his bubble and fight for his attention and understanding. I didn't understand myself. And so began the wedge between us, which only grew bigger the more time we spent not communicating with each other. I resented him for the distance between us. After all, he was the husband. He was supposed to cleave to *me*, not the kids. I was supposed to be his good thing, like Proverbs 18:22 says. I remember crying as I repeated that scripture over and over every night when I was a teenager, asking God to make me somebody's good thing. I never really believed it, so I guess I should've been happy to just be somebody's wife and somebody's mother.

I drew closer to my first love—the church. We looked like a happy family, attending church religiously. We were complete. He had his little girl and I had my little man. So why complain? We had what we'd prayed for. We were complete, right?

When we found out I was pregnant with sweet baby Sydney, I was in shock. I was on the pill. Not that I needed to be since by this time we almost never had sex. While I was dumbstruck, the first thing from my husband's mouth was, "Are you sure?"

What the hell? I was furious. "Listen here," I fired back. "Yes, I'm sure. Why would you ask me that dumb question? I don't care how much you travel and how we can't even spell intimacy. (I was reminded of how one of the church elders broke it down as "intimacy: in-to me, see?") This is your child. And besides, I don't even like dudes like that for real to even cheat on you." Okay, that last line was just in my head. Sydney was born and was the prettiest, chunkiest, pale-colored little baby girl I had ever seen. She was everything to everybody. Even her big brother and sister.

Don't get me wrong. I—we—love our kids—all three of them. They are God's gifts to us. He gave them to us. He knew when we were ready. I'm just not sure we were ready for all the extra. But what couple really is? Things always look great during the courtship. I'm learning that the definition of a working marriage is one that actually does the work when things get messy.

I can't say if he seriously thought I had cheated on him. I

could attribute that to his OCD. When he was diagnosed, his anger and frustration made more sense. He needed everything and everyone in order—his order. Yeah, that didn't go so well. He grew very suspicious of everything I did. It got to the point where I would end a call before coming in the house to keep from being interrogated. It wasn't just annoying it was infuriating.

I shut down and shut him out…Check. Then he began his emotional affairs…Check mate. It was all to get my attention, I realize now. I'd see messages on his phone, or emails. I confronted him each time. He was trying to get me to feel something for him—jealousy, I guess. Oh, I did. But it was a confirmation of how I felt about myself—not him or them. And I couldn't block out Momma's voice in my head: "You're just a fast tail girl, not wife material." I wasn't good enough for him. I could never meet his expectations. Wife material! What is that exactly, but whatever somebody else decides you're supposed to be.

6
Me and She

When it all started, I didn't—couldn't know it would—we would…

We had one thing, or person, I should say, in common—my daughter. She'd seen her play and thought she was phenomenal, especially for her age. She didn't know any twelve-year olds who were that good. Remember, it was Shawn's idea to ask Mel to be my daughter's trainer.

My daughter began training with Mel in the off season of competitive basketball and after a few sessions, she was getting comfortable with her and so was I…too comfortable. At the end of the training season, it was time to try out for a competitive traveling team. She had played for the same team several years but now had an opportunity to play for her trainer. We left it up to her; go back to your old team or join a new one. I was torn about what I wanted her to do. Part of me wanted her to go with the new team but more of me wanted her to go back. A battle between spirit and flesh, good and evil, the voice of reason and the voice of desire. I was able to ignore previous feelings, but I just didn't know if I could do it this time. I was no longer the young pre-teen where my decisions were made for me.

I had my first crush in sixth grade. I remember being so

drawn to her long, straight hair. It was light brown and it looked so much like creamy peanut butter. I went right up to her and sniffed it one day. Even better. It smelled like peppermint. My hair never smelled like that. She said I was weird, but she laughed it off. I wondered what she would do if she knew how I felt. I didn't really know how to express it myself. I felt butterflies every time I got close to her. Would her cute little pink lips taste like cotton candy? I hoped so, but I would never know. I couldn't just reach out and grab her hand, or even hug her. I wasn't sure if she would push me away. I really didn't know what to do.

My first experience with a woman was two years prior. It wasn't my choice. She was a grown woman; someone my parents knew very well. But did they know her well enough to think it was okay for her to put her fingers inside me? I wondered. She was gentle—not like when I was seven. I didn't know ladies did that to girls.

"Why?" I asked her, trembling.

"It's okay, Patti. You're a good girl," she said placing my hands on her breasts. "See, this is nice."

"When will mine get big like yours?" I asked. It was the first time I had seen any that big close up, and the first time I had touched them.

"Pretend these are yours," she said breathing heavily.

"You can do whatever you want."

The only person I told about it was Mel, all these years later. She's the only one who gave me permission to *really feel* what had happened to me. Mel and I talked throughout the week on the phone, between practices. I reminded Shawn I was doing ministry. Counseling her through rough patches in her relationship with her partner; who I didn't even know about until one day she mentioned her out of the blue. I understood the state of their relationship when she started talking about how incompatible they were. Was this jealousy I was feeling? Please! We were just friends, right?

She'd been miserable in the relationship for the past couple of years. So, as a good friend I gave her relationship advice. Sharing with her all the relationship stuff Shawn and I were learning in ministry classes that we weren't applying to our own marriage. We discussed the Bible. I gave her some foundational scriptures and we prayed together. Honestly, I was so focused on our friendship that I didn't see the relationship brewing underneath, at first.

It was so easy to get "caught up" because we spent hours talking about all the things we had in common. We both loved basketball, women's mainly. We could watch and talk about it for hours. We loved all types of music. We both loved family and holidays. We shared things with each other that neither of us shared with anyone else.

It was late September, several months in. I'd shared so much with her by then, bared my soul, really. And she was still here.

"You're such a beautiful and remarkable woman." I read the text over and over. Now my husband had probably told me that a kabillion times, but it sounded and felt so different coming from her.

I played it over and over in my mind, my fingers hovering over my phone. "I'm about to tell you something that's likely to alter our friendship forever."

"Nothing you ever say to me would alter it in a bad way," came her immediate response. I was still nervous. I had no idea where this was going, just that I knew what I felt and I needed to say it.

"I'm beginning to feel something different," I started typing, fingers a bit shaky. "There's more than just a friendship between us. At least, that's how I feel."

Thank God after a split second my phone rang. For the next hour we talked about what that meant.

In her defense, she tried to run as fast as she could in the opposite direction. Although she felt something similar for me, she just couldn't allow herself to think of me as anything other than a really close friend who made her feel a way she had never felt in her entire life.

The next couple of months were interesting. We discussed all the *what-ifs*. What if I wasn't married and she didn't have a partner? What if we'd met years ago? She said I was exactly who she prayed for when she was seventeen. She told me again how beautiful I was and how blessed she was to have me in her life. What if this could really work?

The messages flowed freely and frequently from that point. We'd even sent songs to express how we felt. Maybe love could just be love—pure joy, admiration, appreciation, and acceptance. Finally! I would often tell her that the joy and excitement of waking up knowing I had her in my life washed away all the past, painful memories.

She would call me a walking Hallmark card. Sometimes I was her princess. I pushed aside thoughts of when she used to call me Jenga, like the board game. That was earlier when she expressed that it all felt like a dream and one wrong move could cause it to all come crashing down. I didn't want to think like that. I would talk to her until she felt reassured. But of what?

Our first kiss was literally breathtaking. I was so anxious for it. This would be better than the countdown to Christmas when you could finally unwrap the gifts you'd already found days before. So much better, because it didn't come with that empty feeling the day after Christmas brings. None of the sadness of not getting that one thing you really wanted. She was the only thing I wanted, needed. That soft, tentative kiss became more intense as we both surrendered to it.

I had a momentary flash of the last time I'd been kissed by a girl. It was unwanted. I was being molested at the time. And it left me feeling confused, used and abandoned. Nothing like I was feeling when I gave in to these new emotions. No, this was everything good that I thought I had never deserved.

7

Me, She, and He

You can imagine how life was at home now. My OCD, overly suspicious husband had his discernment meter on 100. I was free (in my mind), loved, and appreciated, just not by him. I was elated. He was pissed. This was pretty much all the time. No doubt the kids were confused. Thinking back, I realize why they never said anything, never asked anything. They just went about their lives and we tried to be as 'normal' for them as possible. Truth is, they probably didn't know what to say. Afraid that might make things worse. No kid wants to see their home, family, everything they know destroyed. No, better to keep quiet and pretend everything was normal.

I probably would've just gone along with that plan, but Mel convinced me that I needed my own space, at least for a while. Our feelings were growing and we needed to see where this was going. I had to be the one to poke the bear. Shawn didn't seem surprised when I told him I was moving out. I needed some space. I had everything planned out, so the kids' schedules were still intact.

"Looks like you have this all figured out," Shawn said.

"It's what's best for everyone for now," I said nervously.

Things had gotten physical between us once before and I was hopeful it wouldn't turn into that. I think I saw some relief in his eyes. Or maybe I was just seeing what I wanted to see. He glared at me.

"Okay, this is what's best for me right now. I am losing my mind, walking on eggshells around you. I need some space to think and get my head together. I hope you can understand."

"You do what you think is best, Patricia. You always do," he said, walking away.

What does that mean? I said in my head. I caught myself. I really didn't want a fight, did I? Or did I want him to fight for me? For us? Nope. He certainly didn't understand me and didn't want to, or so it seemed based on his reaction. So that was that.

I knew I needed to say something to the kids before he did. They didn't need to be in the middle of our mess. (Like they weren't already.) I used my need for space speech again. I assured them it was temporary. That I loved them and we'd both do everything we could to keep their lives running smoothly. I'd see them every day and I would be a happier mom for them. No comments. They must've practiced these poker faces they were giving me. I didn't push it. It was really going to happen.

I got my own place. My own space to breathe, dance, rest, and yes, to see Mel whenever I could. It was surreal. Intimacy was really "in-to me, see!" She wanted to please me, and I recip- rocated. It was like me outside myself, loving myself. Wow!

We prayed, shared scriptures. God was right there, or so I kept telling myself. God gives you the desires of your heart, right? Well, not impure desires silly girl, you're still married. It made it easier for me to continue to live this façade.

Meanwhile, my family attended church regularly. I had stepped down from leadership. The kids were very involved with choir and ushering and Shawn was there as well. Nobody would've guessed what was really going on. And, I guess nobody's discernment was working, because no one even suspected. No one asked. Even people close to us seemed clueless or had excellent game faces. Probably covering up their own issues.

We didn't work too far from one another, so Mel would drop by during the day or I would swing by after work. We saw each other pretty much every day. She'd leave cards at my place when I was away. She bought great gifts. The weekend getaways were great. But leaving me money and blank checks wasn't cool. I needed to be loved, not taken care of by her. I don't think she could distinguish between the two. Maybe it's just that I've never had this. She was so supportive and understanding. She vindicated my seven-year-old, nine-year-old and sixteen-year-old selves. Yeah, she defended me in all my past painful experiences. No one had ever done that. No relationship was perfect. This one was worth fighting for… but at what cost?

We were giddy, carefree, and obviously careless, at least I was. We talked about our first kiss and being intimate for the first time, holding each other---yeah, all that intimate stuff that should've stayed between us was on the Net. Nothing intimate about that. Is that what it means to be drunk in love?

My husband was knee deep in his own distractions; something to help him forget about our situation I suppose. It helped him to mask the pain he was feeling. Pride and ego will make you do unexpected things. That didn't keep him from finding mine and Mel's internet exchanges even after I deactivated my account. Why didn't I think Shawn would find out? Did I want him to? Truthfully, I probably didn't think he'd care enough to become a private investigator but that's exactly what happened.

Road Rescue

I was speeding now and my heart was racing. Confusion

returned. My phone rang. It wasn't that weird ghostly chick again, I hoped. Why would she call when she could just appear beside me? The phone rang several times and I heard: "Pick up the phone. Now!" So, I did.

"Patricia, pull over and stop. I'm coming to get you."

It was my boss from work. How in the world did she…?

"Now. I don't know what you're thinking, but you need to pull off the road," she said, so firmly, I just did what she said.

I did my best to figure out my location and describe it to her. Clearly, I had no idea where I was. I had never been on this road before. I pulled over and began to weep. Once again, I had disappointed the people I loved and I would probably lose the most spectacular thing I ever had. I closed my eyes and thoughts of us flooded my mind.

Passion Playback

"You know you complete me, right?" Mel said, nuzzling the back of my neck. "I was starting to think I was just going to be trapped, just being used up, taking care of her and her kids. I haven't felt like this in…hell, I 've never felt like this. You know what I mean?" she rambled, euphoric in the sweet stillness.

We were at my place…yeah, that's right. My place, my rules. Not exactly. She seemed to always have things her way. Oh, she wasn't demanding or forceful. She just had this way of…well, I guess she just had me open in ways I should've been with Shawn, but I…well, I just wasn't. She let me be me as long as I was who she needed me to be. Not Perfect Patti, like everyone expected. Just me. And that's what I needed. I needed this. Yeah, I was euphoric too.

"I feel the same way," I said, turning to kiss her. I swear, I've never felt anything so soft, slow, passionate, mind-numbing. "But what happens now? Where is this going? How can it…?" I must've wondered aloud.

"Shh!" she said as she placed her finger over my mouth. "You think too much. Turn your mind off and let's just stay in this moment. You always say God is sovereign, so maybe he'll just make this moment last forever."

Okay, that's a really corny song lyric, but I wanted to believe it. For that long beautiful moment I did.

"I love you just the way you are. You're beautiful to me," she continued. Yeah, I know, more song lyrics. But hey, they touched me.

"I love you, too," I replied, like many times before. No guilt, no doubt, no regrets. Maybe because I had shared my most intimate secrets, good and bad, with her—not just the molestations, but my need to be loved. And she told me about tragic times in her life. There was no judgment…just unconditional, pure, everlasting love. I'm smiling now because now I'm hearing those lyrics: *From the very start/open up your heart/Be a lasting part of everlasting love/Real love that will last forever.*

"What's that you're singing?" she asked while gently stroking my back. Wait, I do remember something sweet about Momma. She used to rub my back until I fell asleep. Why did she ever stop being so sweet to me? Was it something I had done?

"Um… Everlasting Love," I said, slightly embarrassed that I was actually singing aloud, not just in my head. "When other loves are gone, ours will still be strong," I sang more boldly now. "We have our very own everlasting love."

"Real love that will last forever," she joined in, though her voice wasn't as strong.

"I've heard that song before. I like it," she said. "That suits us."

"You know every single song made," I said.

She giggled and replied "You know it."

"You sure about that?" I asked, not sure why I should test this. "I'm not talking about knowing every song. I'm talking about our love lasting forever."

"Yeah, aren't you?" she replied so quickly my doubts were almost obliterated.

"Will it last forever?" I asked. "Can it?"

"Patricia, there's no one I want, or have ever wanted, by my side more than you," she said without hesitation. "Now that's real love," she said. "I'm going to marry you and I know exactly how I'm going to propose," she pulled me closer to whisper in my ear.

Back to Life. Back to Reality

"Patti!" someone yelled and knocked on my driver's side window.

"What! Who?" I said startled and snatched from my memory. "You again! Who are you and what do you want?" I yelled, glaring back at my red-haired ghostly nemesis.

"Out with it. I'm sick of you!" I blinked, hoping this was the dream, but when I opened my eyes she was sitting in my car. I grabbed for the handle, but I was actually glad she stopped me. I had no idea where I would have gone in the dark.

"Don't!" is all she said. It was as though she had her hand on my heart. I couldn't move.

"Your help is right here. I've always been right here," she said in that calm soothing voice. "Aren't you tired of running? Don't you know you can't outrun yourself?"

Okay that sounded crazy.

"I'm here to help you if you're ready."

"I don't need your help," I fired back. "My help, my boss is on her way. I just need to breathe and stop tripping."

"Quite true," she said, and faded away.

"I'm losing it," I said, shaking my head. The next knock on my window was my boss.

"Unlock the door!" she called. She seemed more afraid than I was.

"Let's go," she said.

8

My Help Comes

(When I Don't Want It)

Don't judge me. I was grateful God sent my boss to my rescue. I was truly lost out there, but the suicidal thoughts had passed and honestly, I didn't want to be bothered. She took me to her house and I rested and let everyone know I was okay. But over the next few days I was counseled, fussed at, prayed over, begged and bothered. I had half a mind to get back into traffic…maybe without the car this time.

While I was at her place, for which I am grateful, I never saw Mary, the red-haired lady. I had decided I was tripping. Though, strangely, I wanted to see her. Was she an angel? Maybe. I figured God didn't want to talk to me at that time, or maybe I just couldn't hear him.

I used that time to sort some things out. Like how and when did my husband turn into such a good detective? I know it was his discernment, that and Facebook Messenger. No, I normally wouldn't be on any type of social media, private or public talking to my new love about how great her kisses felt and how I couldn't wait to see her again. In my mind there was nobody else when we were together. I had totally surrendered my will to her, and she was gentle with it. Trouble is, when you give yourself totally to someone, what does God get? No wonder He wasn't talking to me. He's a jealous God.

I returned to my apartment to deal with all the backlash of my decision to keep this love I'd wanted my whole life. I actually believed I could have it all. I could have her and somehow keep things civil with husband and my kids. My boss had done all she could. She didn't judge me. And she knew I'd never let my personal life interfere with work, but it actually did.

I knew Shawn was fuming inside, probably about to blow. And then he did. Hurt, furious, sad, sometimes at the same time, he had a straight up "Waiting to Exhale" moment. He actually threw whatever clothes I had left at the house onto the front lawn. Fortunately, he didn't burn them. Unfortunately, an Elder from the church told me about it and wondered what was going on. My family, and the people closest to me had all decided I was going to hell. Well, not all of them. One sister really couldn't say anything, since her daughter had just come out. And one brother was just glad I was still alive. While the other brother said he loved me no matter what, and he was here if I needed him. I needed him to tell everyone else to leave me alone, but I couldn't ask him to do that. I didn't really believe I was going to "bust hell wide open," figuring the power of love was stronger than their curse.

My life, my choice, made perfect sense to me. I was tested and I passed. My closest friend at the time had defended me when Shawn told her about his suspicions way before he had evidence. She told him he was insane. A week later, she reached out to me. Convinced she'd understand, I agreed to meet her for lunch. I talked. She listened and began to understand from my perspective. She couldn't condone the adultery, nor that it was with a woman, but she didn't condemn me. She was going through her own situation. We got closer and became each other's support system. See! I *can* have it all.

"It's an abomination. You're going to hell. Why didn't you feel like you could tell me?" came the resurgence of condemnation from Elizabeth.

Really? Probably because I didn't want to hear any more versions of how I was on the express train to the lake of fire in the pit of hell. How 'bout that! When the guilt got to me (they were relentless) I did get some counseling. I'm not good at dealing with Satan on one shoulder and God on the other. I don't think this is what the song "Crazy in Love" meant. I didn't have any desire to lose my mind, any more than I already had.

I actually had two counselors: my pastor and a psychologist we will call Raymond. My pastor presented the spiritual aspect of what I was going through. Raymond wanted me to see the overall big picture and the possible repercussions of my choices. Pastor was beyond shocked. He had no idea this was going on. And I think if God wanted him to know He would've told him. He said what he was supposed to say and what he believed: that God wasn't pleased. But at that time, I was thinking how could He *not* be pleased that I had found the love of my life. But then he continued, and his response surprised me, too. He told me he loved me and so did God, but God wasn't pleased with my actions.

Hmmm…I listened, trying not to get defensive. He was saying what I already knew, I just didn't always want to hear it. But I was listening now. I had already decided to remove myself from active ministry and he agreed that was best. Using the strength Mel shared with me, I confided to my pastor that I had struggled my entire life with this attraction to women. He didn't flinch.

"I don't want you to leave the church," he said. "In fact, I want to see you sitting in the front row right next to me for every service." He became a big part of my support system.

I loved Shawn because he was my husband and my God covering. He really was a great Godly man. Mel was a lot like him but also very different. Maybe because they had similar, almost identical interests…not just me either. See why I had two counselors?

I felt guilty about a lot of things in my marriage. I really did love Shawn…except when I didn't. Sure, I could just submit, which would make him happy. But what about my happiness! Mel made me feel so good about myself and she was so sympathetic about everything I had endured my whole life. She even took the blame for us, or the fallout from us. No one had ever accepted the blame or responsibility for what had happened to me.

We decided to continue our relationship. The intimacy, not just physical, but the secrets she shared were precious to me. Like the day she came home from school and her life was forever changed. That story helped me understand her need to be the responsible one; why she needed me to be needy because then she would know her role in our relationship. We talked about her attempt to be *normal* by dating a guy. It went against everything in her. I can't even imagine what that would be like. I would never know the courage it took to come out, hoping for acceptance, not persecution.

My whole life was a string of disappointments, misunderstandings, and persecution. I knew I liked girls and could even love one but in my heart I didn't believe I was gay. When I was with her that was all that mattered—just being—no labels.

We had rules, of course. Like, we were never together when I had the kids, though the oldest knew about us. My pride would drown out the guilt of that, most of the time. I was not going to let my child dictate my life. A few family members had rules, too. They decided they'd have nothing to do with me until I came back to my senses. They never missed a chance to tell me I was out of God's will and, therefore, going to hell.

Shawn took a more bipolar approach. One minute he was loving and supportive, not of my lifestyle, but of his faith that I would see that I was better than the life I was living. Yeah, then the next minute he'd be aggressive with me and with her. There's only so much guilt people can heap on you before you start thinking about suicide again. Hurting Shawn, destroying my children, disappointing my family—Perfect Patti was marching into hell wearing gasoline drawers. Trouble is—I'm not even good at taking my own life. Thank God!

9

By Any Means Necessary

I was at the apartment, alone, dealing with everything, I was carving up myself, my guilt, my shame, hurt, and disappointment and serving it up like a pie. There was a big piece for Shawn. I had hurt him to the core. I had cut him so deep that only the blood of Jesus Christ Himself could stop his bleeding. I know that sounds crazy, but it was almost as if a blood transfusion needed to take place. Mel was served a good-sized piece as well. There was a shift in our relationship that I finally noticed. Was she overcome with guilt that caused her to rethink the commitment she made to me?

A piece carved for all the rapes and molestations, one for self-condemnation, for everyone who was shaming me—to my face and behind my back, and, of course Satan got his slice. And that was all there was—I was left with nothing for me. I hadn't slept nor eaten in days. My mind would not turn off. The torture was unbearable. Voices from my past, new ones who joined in—all speaking at once was too much. I just wanted to escape the noise and rest, but I kept hearing the saying "no rest for the weary." And man, was I weary.

I had somehow invited my mother to this pity-party, even though she had passed. I had this burning desire to get it right with her before I took my life—for real this time. It seemed as if I visited every significant conversation and situation that I had with my mother. This time I actually paid attention to her, *listening* rather than just hearing, and not focused on how I was feeling or how what she said was going to affect me. For once, it wasn't about me, it was about her. It was if she was talking about a personal situation rather than the issue at hand. I processed her interaction with my father and my siblings. I recalled stories told about my young mother by my aunts and uncles. She was trying with all she had to give all that she could.

In that very moment, I finally gave myself permission to grieve her passing. After more tears but for different reasons I swallowed all of my anti-depressants for the week, so I could be with my mother. I wanted her to make it all better.

"And when has she ever done what you wanted?" Mary was back. Why I looked under the table I had no idea. But in a blink, she had pulled up a chair and was sitting next to me…or was she? "If you want things to be all better, you know what to do," she said in that familiar, calm voice.

I held out the pill dispenser and prepared to walk into the light. She sat there silently watching as I started to drift. I bet she's the one who is going to take me to my mother. That's it. That's why she was here. She must be the angel of death.

"Girl, please," she said reading my mind. "There is no angel of death. And you're gonna need your stomach pumped," she said shaking her head. Then she did it again. She disappeared. But I didn't. And I realized in that instance that I didn't want to.

I got in my truck and drove while calling my friend/sister/aunt/advisor/cookie. We'll call her Slash… get it? I tried to explain what I'd done. She instructed me to pull over but I was afraid if I did, I would pass out. I asked her to talk to me until

I reached her house on the other side of town. I made it across town, literally by the grace of God. I crossed a busy intersection as the car went into autopilot. I assumed the red-haired ghost was behind the wheel. I didn't have the energy or desire to protest.

Lost and Found

I couldn't tell you how they found me. It was Slash, my husband, and a friend, who was actually my daughter's first AAU coach. Let me just say that God sends the right people at the right time. Although the friend knew what I did; never, not once, did I hear talks about him saying anything about what happened. I am forever grateful for him and to his family. He and Shawn transported me to Slash's car. She drove me to her house, but then decided I should go to the hospital.

My vitals were monitored in the ER where I was pelted with questions by a staff psychiatrist. After several hours I was released…sort of. Slash and her husband took me in for a couple of days. I admit they helped to clear my head. He didn't judge. He told me I was trying to tackle too much on my own. He wasn't wrong. I needed God, and I needed Him bad. I wasn't going to get out of this state alone but my desire and spirit continued to battle.

I somehow connected finding myself, accepting myself, liking myself …with Mel. My *true* feelings may not have been 'true' at all, but just my desperate desire to be loved. You know how a fully-blown balloon is so pretty and buoyant? And if it's full of helium it flies and goes wherever the wind takes it but always going higher and higher. Just like that Jackie Wilson song, "Your Love Keeps Lifting Me Higher." Ever seen a balloon with a slow leak?

One thing I knew for sure about myself…I wasn't needy. Okay, I may be a little crazy, but not needy. She needed me to be needy. And that was the leak. The checks left at my house would be in that same spot when she returned. No one could accuse me of being a gold digger.

"I don't understand why you're with me if you don't need me," she said on more than one occasion. "You pay your own bills, take care of your kids, and never ask for anything. I'm just not used to that," she said shoving the check into her pocket. My counselor explained that was a form of co-dependency. There was a balance there in her current and previous relationships—not a healthy situation, but it worked for her. He believed she loved me in her way, but she didn't know how to truly know and understand me. Did she really want us to have a life together, or was I her breather/side piece? Ouch! Headache. Slow leak.

Next, she'd throw Shawn in the mix. "He's never gonna leave us alone," she'd say. "And I can't afford to fight him."

Did she mean monetarily or emotionally? Or both? Uh… This was her way of telling me it was over, I guess. Fourteen months in and this was it for her? She was so willing to give up on us, just when the hard stuff was coming. I guess that's why most couples, married or not, break up. Me and the hard way were best friends. I guess most people don't think life is supposed to be hard. Just when I was willing to let someone in, someone who I thought would fight the good fight with me…she bailed. Well, mostly.

The next time she came over, we talked for about three more hours—not about anything that really mattered. I felt like she didn't want to put a period on this chapter so she wouldn't look like the bad guy. I was willing to sacrifice my marriage, my family, and damn near everything to be with her. And she—she wouldn't even give up her miserable life with her—whatever she was. She reneged on all her promises and the plans she made for us. I'd given her more of myself than I thought I had. She promised to be gentle with my heart because she knew I'd be gentle with hers. And she told me, aside from her mother, she loved me more than anyone.

I hope you don't kick your mother to the curb, I said in my mind. It was snarky and I didn't want her to know how devastated, used, and foolish I felt. *Honestly, Patti! Hasn't life taught you not to believe empty promises?*

She left and I broke down. I wanted my mother. No, maybe the First Lady. I'd even settle for the red-haired ghost at this point. Crickets…. Once again, I hear the sound of the pesky insect as it's being approached…SILENCE.

"Hello? Somebody? Anybody?", I screamed.

Yes, I hear you loud and clear." I grabbed my head and thought, "here I go with hearing voices again"."It's me. Do you not recognize my voice?"

"Who are you," I responded. The voice sounded somewhat familiar, but no one was appearing.

"My sheep hear my voice. I know them, and they follow me."

"I thought you left me," I responded.

"I will never leave you nor forsake you. You know all this. You've preached it. You've taught it. You've told it to others. You just don't believe it. You left me. I've been here the whole time, loving you, caring for you, protecting you and hearing you when you decide to call out my name."

"Then why am I here?" I croaked, tears flowing again. "Why am I in this place feeling the way I do?"

"Why not you?" God responded. "And why are you serving your feelings?"

Good question. But what type of response was that? I've always been told not to answer a question with a question because it means you're either trying to avoid the question or don't know the answer. Why is an all-knowing God asking instead of answering? In my frustration I repeated, with attitude this time. "WHY AM I IN THIS PLACE?" This time the response was different but honestly, I should have stuck with the first one.

"Because you chose to be here," He replied.

"Pardon me? When did I CHOOSE this? When did I choose to sit in this expensive, tiny apartment by myself holding a handful of lies and broken promises? Tell me Sir, who in their right mind chooses this?"

"No one……in their right mind."

"I'm sick and tired of everyone calling me crazy, confused, and out of my mind."

"Precious, tell me, when did I ever call you those names? I call you *Loved, Beautiful, My Child*. You may do things that are outside of my plans for you but I don't call you crazy. You may not be certain as to who you are but I don't call you confused. You may make decisions without seeking Me first, but I don't say you're out of your mind. I call you *Fearfully and Wonderfully Made*. I think you've forgotten that."

"I quote that every single day to *her*. How can you say I forgot it?"

"Yes, I remind you of your value every day and instead of believing and receiving it for yourself, you think I remind you of that for someone else. I need you to believe all the things you tell her to be true for yourself."

"But God, how can I think those things about me when so many are saying differently?"

"But what do I say? You are far more valuable than rubies. You are loved. You are the apple of my eye. Nothing you could ever do or say would make me leave you."

"Yes, that's what you call me but I don't see myself that way.

It's been one bad hurtful thing after the other since I can remember."

"You have reduced your life to a snapshot in time. You have taken every single bad thing that has happened to you, balled it up and given it to someone who wasn't made to handle you. All the broken places you have within can only be permanently filled by Me, My love, My spirit."

"I wanted you to heal me. I've been looking for you. I've prayed, I fasted, I studied, I meditated. I did it all. But you didn't come."

"The one thing you didn't do was *listen*. I never left you. Everywhere you've gone, I've been there. You've been looking for me and I've been here the whole time. That uncomfortable feeling you get when you are in places you know you shouldn't be, that's me. When the phone call came that kept you from driving into those semi-trucks, that was me. When you left just the right number of pills in the bottle that was me. When you've laid in bed crying until you thought you would lose your sight and you felt a sense of peace, that was me. When you prayed for your husband and children to be protected, I sent My angels to surround them. I've given you space in this situation but I never left you."

In that moment, my heart felt like it was going to explode. I could see situation after situation where God kept His loving arms of protection around me. I could see Him at the road my sister talked about. I was trying my hardest to jump to the other side not realizing the gap was too big for me jump over. There He was holding onto the backpack full of guilt, shame, embarrassment, depression, sickness, lust, rape, molestations, adultery, unforgiveness, feelings of abandonment, and whatever else I was expecting Mel to fix. I was determined to leap but He knew I had gone far past where I needed to be.

I could hear Him say, "Give it to me. Give it all to me. You have kept all that has happened to you in a little box, tucked away thinking it was all done and over with. You pull it out every so often and add to it. Now you've tried to give it away to someone who isn't equipped to handle it and now that she's given it back, you've added great disappointment to the collection. Hand it over, give it to me so you can start walking toward your destiny."

There was a peace that came over me that I surely can't explain. The whole time He was talking but because I was so self-absorbed and doing my own thing, I couldn't hear Him. I had an epiphany. It wasn't earth shattering. I just suddenly realized—no, God showed me, and I was paying attention that day. I wrote the word *freedom* at the top of a page I had intended to be a letter to place in my box. God had another plan. Beneath the word I wrote down the names of everyone in my life who needed me—everyone I felt the need to please. I really did love them and I had told myself my purpose was to be my best for them. But I never heard God say that. Next, I added the names of those who violated me, stole from my innocence, and took advantage of me. As I wrote the names, tears began to flow down my cheeks. With each teardrop, I forgave each of them.

God told me to look at the list—this crazy long list. Then I heard Him say "You can't do this, you know. Look at this. It'll make you crazy."

Then I heard laughter. Whose voice was it? My mother's? That red-haired, apparition? No, it was me. I was cracking myself up. "You're right," I said through tears of delirium. And this was without wine. "I can't do this."

"Not on your own," He said. "But in my strength you can be free to love—not please—but to love. You are free to be your best self—which is exactly who you are—yielding every moment to Me. I like who I made you to be, who you have become. And I love your spirit—your essence—your personality. Can you love me enough to accept this? By the way, it's free, with My promise of more to come.

"Hmm," I thought. All this time I was fighting for something that was free? Freedom really meant being free to choose God and to accept his acceptance of me. He loved me as *Perfect Patti, hot-mess Patti,* and every phase in between. I suddenly realized the only way I could be a good mother was to allow God's freedom to guide me and His strength to empower me to get through the challenges. I'd start there and see how it went. If this didn't work, I wouldn't be any worse off than I am right now. But what if this really does work; what if I take Him at His word, for real this time?

"Yes! Yes! Yes!" I said as a peace washed over me. This is what I'd been hoping for all my life. I thought I had found it in Mel but at this point, all I wanted to say was, "I surrender all." The spirit of the Lord filled every single void in me. I sang out loud, sitting on my apartment floor: "All to Jesus, I surrender. All to thee I freely give." There it was again, freedom. No longer in bondage. On my way to being all that I was called to be. I was able to say "Lord let my will line up with Your will. Nothing more, nothing less!" Along with the renewed peace I was experiencing, I knew the enemy was coming with both barrels loaded.

As I drifted off to sleep for the first time in a couple of days, I dreamt of my mother. Not just any ordinary dream but one that was conversational in nature.

"Mommy, can you rub my back?"

"Of course. Come lay your head on mommy's lap."

Although I was grown, she never said no when I wanted a

back rub. When I was little, she used to put me to sleep by rubbing my back. It was the most soothing thing ever.

"Can we play cards tonight with Aunt D and have hot tea?"

"Sure, after dinner and the kitchen gets cleaned."

Why didn't I remember great times like this more often? I tended to focus on the things she didn't do. Actually, I formed my opinion because she wasn't there to protect me when I needed it. But how could she if she never knew. But shouldn't a mother know when her child is hurting? Isn't there an instinct that comes the moment you experience child birth? I was the youngest of eight for crying out loud. I can see the first, second, and maybe even the third but *geez.*

"Mom, why didn't you really love me?"

"Patti, are you serious?"

"Absolutely! I never felt like you loved me. I always felt you tolerated me and didn't want to be bothered with me."

"I loved you more than I could ever tell or show you. I loved your brothers and sisters too. Why didn't you ever just stop to consider that everything I did was out of love for each of you? All I could do was what I did my whole life—love you through my pain. Press on to give everything to you all, even when I was empty."

"But what about when I was hurting?

"Patti, people go through hurt, disappointment—even abuse. It's called life."

"So that's it? I'm just supposed to suck it up and get over it? All of those years of…"

"I didn't want bad things to happen to you, Patti. My mother wouldn't have wanted that for me either but she wasn't there. I hated to see you go through – experiencing the same as me, because I knew that pain all too well."

"You knew? Why didn't you just tell me?" I asked through stream of tears. "You never talked to me. I thought you didn't even like me."

"I didn't know specifics but I could tell you were hurting. I did what I thought would help you and talking about the awful things that happened to me wasn't going to help you or me. You're going to realize one day that it's how you get over it and move on, is what you need to show—not to tell your children details of the horrific things that happened to you."

"Just get over it? Whatever *it* was. I still don't know exactly what you went through. Some things you can't just get over, Mother!" I said with more anger than I intended.

"Let me make this clear, Patricia. You don't need to know everything. How is that going to help you now? What you need to know—to learn—is you get over it—well, maybe I said that wrong. You get over it by giving it to God and moving on. You trust Him with all that pain. You darn sure don't wait for somebody to apologize because that's not going to happen. And even if it did, you wouldn't feel any better. Trust me on that. I think God sees to it so we have to trust Him and His grace."

After a long pause, she added, "Despite what you think, I did love you. I gave you and the others all I had. I couldn't give you what I was never taught, given or experienced. I gave you what I thought you needed most of all, and that was Jesus."

"I know," I whispered. "And I'm grateful for that. I love you too, Mommy!"

I began to realize that my mother was not as bad and evil as I once thought. She had been through her own encounters with abuse. She experienced loss well before she even knew her life existed. Her mother died two weeks after her birth and her father was murdered when she was young girl. A grandmother who was only able to give her what she had to give and, hence, my mother could only give what she had been given. As a mother, I must do better than the generations before me.

Then I felt her leave. The next morning (I mean afternoon) when I woke, I was drained but determined to prepare myself for whatever the world was going to throw at me for the day. This time, I was better armed.

10

Side Chick

Although I had that life-shifting encounter with God and my mother, it was still really hard to let Mel go. And let me tell you this, it was hard to admit when I realized I was the side chick, y'all. Visits were less frequent. Getaways had ceased. Meals were at home now and we hardly talked, but baby, that soul tie was no joke. I had not only given my heart, will and mind to her, I gifted my soul to her as well. When we are intimate with someone, it's more than just a physical thing that takes place. Your souls unite. Everything you do, think, say, and feel is driven by that person and it's hard as hell to let go.

I spent more time alone than I had ever anticipated. I suppose I was living what I spoke. "I need a space of my own. I need time to gather my thoughts. I feel smothered and controlled." God said, "Ok, I got you." He's such a comedian.

One Saturday while the kids were with their dad, I went to hang out with two of my closest friends. One was on a very similar journey and the other was part of our support system. While there, I became very ill. I went to the bathroom and the blood flowed uncontrollably. It looked like a true SVU crime scene. I was terrified. I yelled out to my friends, "Help me please!"

They both came busting through the door. "Oh, my goodness, Patricia. What happened?" I had no idea. Now Lord knows I wasn't pregnant. THAT would be a miracle. All I know is I went to use the bathroom and the blood of Jesus I always prayed to flow through my veins, had made its way all over my friend's bathroom floor.

After cleaning up, speaking to the nurse and changing my clothes, which was comic relief because my friend was smaller than me, I gathered my things and went "home." Although I left it and hadn't always felt it, home was now my safe place. At this point there was a shift in the atmosphere and it was one of the more peaceful places I could be. God was up to something and he was getting my attention by any means necessary. I tell people that all the time. God gives you chance after chance after chance. Warning after warning after warning. Then comes the "situation" and that typically blows your mind.

The nurse had given me some instructions and one was to make an appointment with my OB/GYN. I did as she instructed and made my way to the doctor that Monday. After the examination she explained that I needed to have a procedure done so that a biopsy could be performed.

Then I went to get the results. "Come again! What did you just say to me?"

When my doctor spoke the words "cervical cancer" my stomach dropped to the ground. She also said that I had multiple fibroids that needed to be removed. That is what caused the massive bleeding and lead to the discovering of the cancer. A complete hysterectomy was in my future.

I knew I had to focus on me. I needed to go home. I still didn't want to but I was facing several weeks of recovery and living alone wasn't gonna cut it. No way my son was going to let that happen. He was so protective of me. Okay, I *am* needy. And where was

Mel now? Why in the halibut did I care? That is what a soul tie does to you.

I told a handful of people about the cancer: Shawn, Slash, the two friends who assisted me during the first scene of my horror movie, and a couple I met through Mel. These ladies were amazing and I'm glad we became close friends. I'll call them *billable* and the other *non-billable*.

As I was coping with these new issues, I was still torn between what I wanted and what I needed. My mind still wanted Mel but my soul was crying for freedom: freedom with God. Honestly, I struggled and struggled bad.

"Now Patti Dulin, you are worth so much more than how she's treating you," *billable* said in her calm, sweet voice. "God has a beautiful plan for you, and I don't see her in it. I know you're hurting right now, but in time you'll realize everyone isn't capable of handling all the love you have to give. You know, the unconditional kind. You're gonna be just fine. You'll see. You need to focus on your health right now anyway."

"Get your sh*t together, girl," *non-billable* added. "She's changed. Your girl is a player and unfortunately, you've become a part of the game; she wants to have her cake and eat it too. If she wants to be miserable in her hopeless situation, let her. Stop wasting your energy, love, and tears on someone who isn't worth it. Don't make me hop in my car, drive to you, and poke your heart-eyes out!"

Total opposite personalities, but they both have such good hearts. *Billable* offered to come and stay with me during recovery, but they lived ten hours away. I couldn't expect her to do that. These ladies were very instrumental in my decision to go home, saying that Shawn was a good man. Now how in the world would they know that unless their conclusion came from the things I told them about him? God wastes nothing and will use whoever is willing to be used. They said he would take care of me and love me through this. I knew he would. I was still on this emotional rollercoaster, fueled by anger, hurt, fear, embarrassment, condemnation, and some other stuff I didn't even want to deal with. I couldn't decide which emotions connected with her and which to Shawn. So, I just cried…and cried and cried some more.

I fantasized about how Mel would react when I told her about my health situation. How she'd fold me in her arms, stroke my hair, and whisper that we'd get through it together. That she'd take care of me in sickness and in health. Hey, don't judge me. I didn't come up with these fantasies all by myself. I was gullible and believed every single promise that ended up shattered. And I really wanted to still hope. Still believe that somehow this would turn into a beautiful life for us.

But I didn't have to call her. She called me.

"Hey," Mel said, hesitantly. "I hadn't heard from you in a few days, so I was just checking in." I've always hated when she said that. You're not my parole officer.

"Hey, yourself," I replied, keeping my thoughts inside. "How are you?"

I didn't really want to know, but I needed to buy some time. Truth is, I missed hearing her voice. I missed a lot of things about her.

"Uh, you know. Just finished my "honey do" list and figured I deserved a reward." And there it was. I could feel her self-satisfied smile, complete with the dimple, through the phone. I was her Scooby snack, her treat. Her reward for doing whatever her partner had been nagging her to do.

"I have cervical cancer," I blurted out. "I'm going to undergo surgery. I'd appreciate your prayers." I had a lifetime to ponder what I'd just said. What did I expect *her* to say? Maybe that she'd be right over? Then what. The silence on the other end really wasn't helping. Finally, I could hear her exhale. Still no clue what was to come.

"Oh, God," she said. "I am so sorry, princess. I wish there was something I could do. I remember how I was when I had surgery. I don't know what I would have done if I had been alone. Everybody was so surprised at how quickly I recovered, though. I was back at work in a week. But everybody's different, I guess. You know if I could be there I would, but things are still a little tense here at times. And with my job, I couldn't just go to the hospital. You know I have people there, right. Imagine if they found out about us. Our friendship. It's still a little complicated."

Our friendship? What the hell type of friendship leads you to believe you're going to spend the rest of your life with someone. What were we going to do forever? Be on a never-ending girls' trip. GIRL, BYE! The more she talked, the more pissed off I became at myself for getting mad at her because of the expectations she would never able to reach.

All that back-peddling through B.S. was about to give me a stroke. Somehow, someway, every conversation ended up being about her! How was I so blind? The Lord had removed the scales from my eyes or maybe *billable* rode through with a needle and deflated my heart eyes. I suppose in the beginning it was wonderful having someone who would share her life, job, feelings, etc. Shawn was and still is the quiet type. He gains a better perspective by listening than talking. Mel confided that no one had ever been interested in actually knowing who she was or how she felt.

I recall asking her once, "What do you like? What makes you happy? What do you dream about?" You would have thought I was a genie who just told her she had three free wishes.

She was stunned and after asking her what was wrong, she replied, "No one has ever asked me that before."

"So, you reassured your partner that you are being faithful I'm sure," I said, sounding like Counselor Troy of the Star Trek Enterprise.

"Yeah, but you know I have to continue to reassure her. She's still jealous of you, even knowing we're just friends now. It's actually kind of cute. We're still working on stuff. I can't have her messing things up for me at work. You know she could make a scene if she wanted to. I'm just not gonna give her any reason to. But it's hard sometimes when your heart wants what it can't have."

"Yeah. I know. All you can do is keep doing those 'honey do's.' I'm sure it'll get better. And I'll be fine, too," I said, fuming and hurt and jealous and—just exhausted.

"I know you will. You still inspire me. You know that, right? I'm so much better as a person, a partner. I owe you so much, Patricia. I really do."

"And you owe her, too," I replied. "That's why you're there and not here, right?"

"Yeah. She needs me. They need me. We've been through this. If things were different…"

"I know. If things were different," I sighed.

"Who's going to care for you?" she asked.

"The same person who has always cared for me." Okay, I must admit I was being petty in this response because I hadn't even told him about it yet.

"Shawn?"

"Yep. That's the plan," I said. What was this? Jealousy?

"Good. I know he'll take good care of you," she said. Okay, not jealousy.

"Well, thanks for calling," I said, hoping to disguise the tremor in my voice.

"When is your surgery?" she asked. I felt like she was just trying to keep me on the phone.

I rolled my eyes and replied, "I'll let you know when and keep you posted on my recovery."

"You better," she said. "I just want the best for you. You deserve it and you know I'll always love you."

"Thanks. Bye," I said, clicking off and throwing the phone across the room. It thankfully landed on the couch. I sat and let my mind wander. Why, God? Can't you just make her disappear, like go away forever?

"No one made you answer that phone call," came the reply.

When I told Shawn what was going on, he cried. We had divorced by then, so I wasn't sure what to expect. I really just wanted to know if I could come home to recover.

"This will always be your home," he said. "Just let me take care of you through your recovery. I don't expect anything in return." I was so grateful for him for so many reasons.

The next day I went to the house at lunch to take a nap because I was exhausted. While lying on the couch, he covered me with a blanket and kissed me on the forehead. Then he listened, no judging, no unsolicited advice. I must have drifted off to sleep because he woke me and said, "It will get better. Everything will be fine." He prayed for me and I headed back to work, thinking, feeling, and allowing myself to feel love from him. Years later, he would divulge that he knew what had upset me that day. He could see the brokenness on my face. He tried to give me the love I wanted from her.

11

The Loooooonnnng Road Home

Don't start picturing a Hallmark movie with a Tyler Perry ending. The road ahead was quite rocky. Nearly every day my mind went back to that red-haired ghost asking me what I wanted. You'd think after everything I'd endured, and having time to sort it all out, the answer would be crystal clear. Yeah, you'd think.

Oh, I knew it wouldn't be a cakewalk. I didn't know how hard it would be to walk on eggshells while healing physically and wondering how my spiritual healing would pan out. I was still fighting not to fall into my default Perfect Patti mode. I hadn't realized how much Shawn and the kids had come to expect that. It must've made them feel like everything was going back to normal. Their normal was so far from mine. How could I give them what they wanted, maybe needed from me? Would it mean losing myself after I fought so hard and was still fighting, to find my true self.

And what, or who did God want me to be? When I asked myself that question in the hospital, shortly after surgery, I could sort out my thoughts. I could pray during the intermissions, after one nurse would leave, before another came in to check something. I could hear myself breathing in and out and it soothed me. That alone told me God was working in me, keeping me alive, strengthening me for act two. I could actually hear my spirit crying out to Him. And, at times, I heard Him telling me how much He loved me.

In my mind I tossed and turned that first night at home. I couldn't really move much because it was so uncomfortable. Every position hurt like hell, so I just laid like a corpse, praying sleep would come. Of course, it did, just as everyone was getting up to start the day. They were all very attentive and sympathetic. I couldn't help thinking that any day someone would say, "Okay, get up now. It's time to get back to normal." The pampering would cease and I'd be covered in piles of soiled laundry and dirty dishes.

I remember drifting off one afternoon. I blame it on the medication. One minute I was just drifting on a peaceful sea under blue skies with a mild breeze whispering to myself, "All is well." Soon the sky turned black, the wind whipped up and I was spinning, like I was being flushed down a huge toilet. I called out for help, but there was no one. I held onto the sides of the boat and called "Peace, be still," over and over.

Fish started flopping up onto the boat: slimy, stinky, talking fish. I should've known it was a dream, but I couldn't wake myself. Still spinning. Now the fish were perching (no pun intended) on their hind fins and pointing their front fins accusingly at me.

"What kind of mother are you?" one of them squealed.

"Yeah," another one added. "This place is a mess. You better get crackin'."

"You're drooling," a giant goldfish chimed in. "When are you going to comb your hair?"

"And you smell worse than me," a huge catfish added. "You should really jump in the lake."

"You better be a strong swimmer," a salmon commented from the water below. "It's not easy swimming upstream, against the current. You're much too weak. If you jump, you'll get flushed down the crapper, just like a—"

"Enough!" the red-haired lady snapped. She was dressed like a fisherman. She was rowing now, trying to turn the boat in the opposite direction. "Are you really just going to sit here and spin and take this?"

"I don't know what else to do," I cried. Now I knew I was dreaming. I would not be in this boat, first of all. And I would definitely not be crying while some funky fish insulted me and tried to make me drown.

"Wake up. Wake up. Just freakin' wake up!" I shouted.

"I know that's right," the red-haired lady said. "Wake up, girl. Grab these little funky bastards and throw them overboard. Just like this," she said, snatching one by the fin and tossing it over the side.

"Hey, you can't do that," the little fish protested leaping up, then splashing back into the water.

"That's right," the goldfish said, pointing at me. "She's supposed to do it. But she's too perfect. Afraid to get her hands dirty. She won't touch me. She's too sca—" Before I could think, I pinched its fin and tossed it over the side.

"Good show," the red-haired lady said, clapping.

"That was nothing," the big catfish crooned. "You're weak and dirty and smelly. Your past made sure of it. You're a bottom feeder, just like me. Except I can adapt. But not you. No, you just conform. You're just the way they want you to be. You're a chameleon. You're just content to wallow in your mess. You're not Perfect Patti. Messy Patti. Hot-mess Patti. Pathetic Patti," he said flipping up in the air, then landing upright on his tail on the floor of the boat.

Was he right? I knew I didn't want to be Perfect Patti, but I didn't know how to change. Not like a chameleon. I mean really changed into—into who?

"I know you're not going to let this three-piece dinner read you like this," the red-haired lady said, standing, hands on her hips.

"What can I do? He's right," I said.

"Do what you do," the red-haired lady said, packing up her belongings, as if she was about to leave. "Clearly you're not ready," she said, zipping her pack. "It's like when you catch a fish that's just too small to do anything with. It's not ready for frying, so you unhook it and toss it back."

"What do you mean? Are you tossing me back?" I said, tears forming. "Don't go!"

"What if I fall in? The salmon was right. I'm not much of a swimmer. Whoa!" I said as the boat rocked more on the choppy water.

"It's not about how strong a swimmer you are.

You really are—'Stuck on You," she sang, sounding a lot like Lionel Richie. "And that catfish had a point, too. You're scared. Scared to jump. Scared to stand. Scared to swim. You're worse than Peter. At least he was brave enough to step out of the boat. Where's your faith, Patti?"

The boat was spinning more. I wanted to lean over the rail to puke, but I knew if I turned away, she'd leave me here alone. I held on to the side, swallowed slowly and stared at her with pleading eyes. I couldn't figure out why she could stand perfectly still while I was holding on for dear life. I could barely hear her now, past the ringing in my ears.

"What do you think will happen if you jump? Don't answer. Your first and only thought is that you'll drown; that you'll get flushed away. Maybe God wants you to take a leap of faith." And with that, she leapt over the side and disappeared.

"Jump, jump! The catfish'll make you jump, jump," my tormentor chanted. I knew what he was doing—trying to make *me* do. So, I joined in. We made a really weird version of Kriss Kross. "Some of them try to rhyme, but they can't rhyme like this. Some of them try to rhyme, but they can't rhyme like this."

"Cause I'm the kickety, kickety, kickety, kitckety cat—fish," he said, flipping and jumping. "And I'm out," he said before flipping back into the water, making a huge splash that splattered on my nightgown. "Too bad you couldn't catch me," he said before swimming away, deep into the water.

The waters calmed and the boat stopped rocking. I thought I was safe now. That I could just drift until… I don't know. Until someone came on a much bigger boat, maybe a yacht, to rescue me.

As if on cue, I heard the loud whistle as the yacht approached. I could see her at the bow, waving and smiling. I knew she'd come. Thank God!

"I love you," I shouted, standing and waving back. The yacht picked up speed, getting closer and closer, but not slowing down. She was close enough to hear me, so I called again. "Slow down. Where's the life raft, or ladder or something for me to climb?" She didn't answer. No, I could see she wasn't looking at me, but past me. The yacht swerved skimming the side of my little boat, going full speed ahead. I turned to see where she was headed, just as my boat capsized.

"Help," I said, desperately trying to remember how to swim.

"Jesus, help me!" But help didn't come. Then something brushed me. Please, God, not a shark. I glanced to my left and saw it was my yellow flower box. What was it doing here? Did God send it? Was there something inside that could save me? I reached for it but it disappeared. Or washed away, I guess. "Someone, help me. Please!"

The phone rang and I jumped up, drenched, wondering if I had really been drowning. "Hello!" I said, breathless. "Princess, what's wrong? Are you okay?" she said, with serious concern in her tone. "I was just calling to check on you. What's wrong?" "Why didn't you save me? Where did you go? I nearly drowned and you just sped past."

"Calm down. Help me out here. They must have you on some really strong meds. Do you need me to—um… Sounds like you had a nightmare. You know I'm always here for you, right? Take a deep breath and tell me how you're feeling."

I took that breath and pulled the covers up around me. No boat. It was the meds. We talked for what seemed like hours. For the first time in a long time, she didn't mention her partner, her job, Shawn, or even herself. It was so hard to say goodbye. (Yeah, another song reference.) I knew as soon as I did, the walls would close in on me.

By the time I had showered and tried to look as good as I was feeling, it was nearly five. Everyone would be home soon. "Oh, shoot!" I told Shawn if I felt well enough, I'd make dinner that night. Not what I wanted to do at all, but I figured God would want me to and the family had been hinting about my spaghetti and garlic bread.

They were greeted at the door by a smiling me, hair combed, smelling good—not at all like smelly fish. The aromas of garlic and parmesan wafted through the house and made everyone smile as they cleaned up for dinner. Conversations were light and lively. I was in a bit of pain, but I covered it well.

I couldn't help noticing Shawn's silence. Bad day at work I guessed. He'd probably tell me about it after the kids went to their rooms. And, man, did he ever!

"You don't want this and you don't want to be here," he said softly, but I could feel the anger bubbling beneath each word.

"What are you talking about?" I asked, honestly blind-sided. I knew Shawn's discernment could be uncanny, but I kept my composure, or tried to.

"I guess this stronghold will take more prayer. I'll get on that tomorrow. Tonight, I'm just gonna be pissed. I'm not gonna share my bed with you and her tonight. I'll be on the couch." Wow! How does he do this? How could he know? And how much did he know?

"You didn't fool any of us, FYI," he said with an impish grin that now had me confused. You had one job today, Patti, that you volunteered to do. I guess we should be thankful you took your thoughts off her long enough to call Romano's and order dinner. I guess you didn't have time to take the containers out to the trash. The kids thought you had over extended yourself and were trying to save face to give us a nice dinner. Nobody busted you."

"But I know exactly what God showed me," he continued.

"I can't let you flaunt your affair in my face in our home. I told you this would always be your home, and I meant that. But I won't have these spirits in this house aroound my kids."

"They're my kids, too," I said. "And I am trying. I am trying to be everything God wants me to be to everybody in this house."

"But, as I said, you don't want to do this. You're not ready—"

"To go back to being what everyone else wants and needs, no matter what I want. Is that it, Shawn?" I said.

"To submit to God, become who He wants you to be," he said, trying to mask his anger and disappointment.

"You'll never truly be happy until you do that. She can't give it to you, I can't give it to you, even YOU can't give it to you."

He may have great discernment, but his eyes don't lie. I could see the hurt in them and I had no idea what to do about that. And yes, a big part of me was tired of this conversation and this life. This couldn't be God's best for me—not even for him again.

"You don't want this either," I blurted out. "So why are we playing this same old tired song? Nobody wants to sing this anymore."

"You're right," he said. "I don't want THIS. I want what God has for us and this family. You have to decide if that's what you want."

How could there ever be a question as to what I want? What is wrong with me? Am I seriously entertaining the thought of continuing anything with this person? Man or woman; she is not good for me. Why is there still a battle between my heart, head and soul? My soul, I had surrendered to God. My head was trying to focus on Shawn, our children, and our home. My heart was still with her. I was right back to square one. My emotions were all over the place.

The faith I had built looked different. I didn't want to leave, but I didn't know what to do. I cried myself to sleep that night. Not over her, not over Shawn but, yes, over myself. I finally realized that I had lost myself, family, friends, status, positions, reputation, hair, weight, just about everything. I had compromised who I was becoming for what I thought I wanted. What I wanted, no needed to know was who I really was. I'm sorry God, but I need to know now.

My main problem was I needed to give my heart, mind and soul to God. I hadn't surrendered all to Jesus, as the song says. I knew I was holding back. Was it fear? Duh! "Okay, God. I'll just do it afraid, until the fear goes away." There were more tests along the way and I developed a habit of seeking God first. I started looking at Shawn as my parenting partner. We were always civil now. With freedom, I noticed the absence of fear. When we agreed to tell each other everything, no holding back, to be completely transparent and trust our feelings to God, I actually believed we could do it. It was hard for both of us. We're so competitive, neither wanted to lose, so both of us were winning. We had this parenting thing on lock. The relationship thing would take more time.

He tried to understand my feelings for her and I tried to tolerate his responses to feeling emotionally abandoned and disconnected at times. Although at times I became frustrated, I knew I could not place a timeframe or parameters around his healing. When emotions flared, we'd go to our neutral corners and talk to God. Sometimes it would take a few days for us to communicate with each other about the situation, but during those times I really missed my friend. I daydreamed about the good times, like when we first met. He told me he knew I was the one for him. That he admired my relationship with God.

He knows I'm also still working through my feelings about *her*. He has my permission, since he asked, to express his feelings at times and at other times just to be silent. He suggested we pray together about it. I agreed, but I have to remind myself every day that I can't be afraid when God totally removes her from my life. If I had only listened to Him in the beginning, or run, maybe I wouldn't be in this mess. But I would've missed this special opportunity to really have intimacy abiding with God. I would've missed trying God and allowing Him to be strong in my weakness.

I'm honest with God and Shawn about her. This experience is helping me to see the God in Shawn. As much as it hurts, he's determined not to feel jealousy. He is a good, Godly man. He's *my* man. I love how saying that makes me feel giddy.

12

There's No Place Like Home

It's covenant day. Pastor said we should have an actual ceremony. "You've both been purified in the fire through this journey. Your minds are renewed, so this is a time to celebrate a new thing," he said.

That sounded good to us. Not like the first time, but better, like Pastor said. I was still working on phase two, trusting God with the marriage. Clearly God was the only one who could fix it.

This reminded me of when my favorite doll broke, my father glued her back together. She never talked anymore—well, she did, but it didn't make a lot of sense. I didn't throw her away. In fact, I loved her even more because I knew she needed me. I didn't expect the same sound or words, and I was okay if she couldn't blink her eyes anymore. She was still mine. I thought about that when I walked up the aisle to stand beside Shawn in the sanctuary that day. I saw or felt his eyes—God's eyes—looking at me with acceptance and unconditional love; like he couldn't wait to love me—not again, but anew. And I was ready to let him.

Only Pastor, his wife, and our 'go-to' Elder were there—well, that's who was there in the natural. I didn't flinch when I glanced over to see the red-haired lady sitting on the front pew in all her finery. I expected to see her. How her hair was still blowing like a shampoo commercial, when there was no wind, I had no idea.

That night I had a dream that made me sit up, get up and reach for my box with the yellow flower. Shawn was sound asleep, I thought. I don't know why I thought I could sweep away all the residue from the past. You can be a new creature, but you still have battles. Through my tears, bits of the dream filled my head. It was a boxing ring. Uh, I am not into boxing. I have never boxed. Why couldn't this be a basketball dream? Sorry, God. I forgot I don't run this show, You do.

I was in one corner and I was getting the snot beat out of me. My eye was swollen, nearly shut. I couldn't even see my opponent. Was it Shawn? Mel? My mother? My cousin? My play cousin? The Woman? The Youth Pastor? I don't know what round it was. I looked around at everyone who was cheering and shouting, "Get back up and finish, Patricia!" I knew these people—family and friends from every phase of my life. Some had signs, but I couldn't make out the words. I was dizzy and probably should've stayed down for the count, but apparently, I didn't have that option, since I was sitting on this little stool in the corner.

She cut me just below my eye to allow the blood to flow. Good thing I was loopy, with spaghetti arms and legs, or I'd have tried to knock her out. I sat there, letting my cut man or woman, rather, tend to my wounds.

"Just one more round," she said reading my mind. The competitor in me just wanted to finish. I am not a quitter. "Lead with your left. And duck more," she said looking at my face that felt like ground beef.

"R O G! R O G!" I heard the chant growing.

"What are they saying? What is ROG? Is that who I'm fighting?" I asked, as the red-haired lady shoved my mouth guard back in.

"That's you," she said pulling me to my feet. "You're the Righteousness of God." She pushed me out to face my opponent. I couldn't tell if it was male, female, black or white. It was huge. And mad. It swung and I ducked. I tried to think of how to lead with my left, but I didn't think that would help, since this fighter punched me in the gut.

"Help me," I cried bending. "Why won't somebody help me?" It was the dead silence in this gym or arena, or wherever—that woke me. My shaky hands managed to lift the lid off the box as tears hit the faded flower I had drawn a lifetime ago. I don't know what I was hoping to find. I opened every letter, every poem, every prayer and found the same thing: a big red check mark across each page, blocking all the words, all the pain, all the doubts and fears.

"It's done," I heard. Just that quickly, I was back in the ring, on the floor in the fetal position. Then I heard the count. I had seen enough Rocky movies to know I better get up before he counted to ten. But how? "Get up!" I yelled. My body wasn't listening.

"Use your renewed mind," she said so softly I don't know how I heard over the crowd chanting "It's done!"

"You're the R O G," she reminded me.

"I am," I said. "God, I need you."

"You're wearing my armor," He said. "Now get up and claim your victory."

I did. I was up on my feet. Don't ask me how. I saw my opponent, back turned, jumping up and down in celebration. I ran toward it, just as it whirled around. I was ready. I don't know which hand, right, left? I swung with everything in me and I connected, right on the mouth. Its mouthpiece flew out and blood spurted all over me. Sounds sick, but it actually felt good. Maybe because this time my opponent was on the ground and not moving. I didn't celebrate. I waited and counted with the ref and everyone else. Shawn ran into the ring and helped place the champion belt on me. I collapsed in his arms and heard him say, "Now let's get ready for the next one—together."

13
Hindsight

When I began to form the pages of this book, I was in a good place physically, mentally, and most of all spiritual. I have been able to process every emotion thoroughly. I know that everything I did, and everything that happened to me outside of God's intentions was used to get me where I am supposed to be; on the journey to my God given destiny. I learned lessons that had an undeniable impact on me. God does not waste anything if you hand it over and allow Him to use it. We must acknowledge His presence, accept His love and recognize His power.

When I thought God wasn't there, He was there the whole time and in control. Envision yourself holding a ball in your hand with your other hand directly below the one holding the ball. The ball is just slightly bigger than your hand, therefore it's unstable. While rolling the ball in your hand, it eventually falls, but not to the ground, into the hand underneath. The ball is representation of your life.

The hand that holds the ball represents YOUR thoughts, plans, decisions. You can control the ball for a certain amount of time and when you can't sustain it any longer, it falls into the hands of God. Freewill allows us to make choices, and whether good or bad, God's got us. Sometimes we get yanked like we're attached to a bungee cord and we're stretched to capacity. That's when God says, "Okay, that's far enough." Going through my wilderness journey helped me realize my decisions had caused a disconnect with God. I missed the warning signs. I concluded this was people trying to make me conform to their expectations. It was actually pride. I wanted to be right.

Each person played an incredibly significant part during the time in my wilderness. I now see that each person was strategically placed throughout the process: my sisters, my pastor, my counselor, my supporters, my critics, those rooting for me to rise, and even those praying that I stay down.

The cricket has been put away; the tears of guilt, shame, and condemnation have dried up and I am now walking in my "Fearfully and Wonderfully Made" truth. Struggles come and struggles go but what has changed within me this time is that I know who I am and whose I am….and THAT makes all the difference in the world.

Prayer

Dear Heavenly Father,

I come to you in the matchless name of your son Jesus Christ thanking you for another day. I pray right now that every distraction and plan set to take our attention from you would not succeed. I thank you for a divine purpose in the lives of the reader and myself. I thank you that not one weapon designed against us shall come to pass.

Oh Lord, I thank you for loving me unconditionally. I thank you for loving me even when I was spiritually incapable of loving myself. I thank you for loving me when many felt I was unlovable. Thank you for delivering me from the hands of the enemy and everything that once held me bound.

Lord, I pray for every person who reads this manuscript. I pray that what you've brought me through encourages them to push pass the pain of their past in pursuit of their true purpose. I call them, blessed, delivered, and free from all that has held them captive spiritually and emotionally. Lord, I thank you that the reader understands everything that has happen to them by their own hand or by the hands of others does not define who they really are and who you created them to be. Lord, I thank you for what they understand and believe: Psalm 139: 14, they are fearfully and wonderfully made. Give them the courage to fight against everything in them that is not like you. When they feel life closing in, let them remember you can be and are the center of their joy. You bring perfect peace in the midst of the greatest storms.

Father God, you are so merciful and great. Thank you for sending your son Jesus to die for us so that we may live again. Thank you as you continue to bless us far beyond what we could ever think or imagine. For it is in your son's precious name we pray, amen.

* *

Prayer of Salvation

While reading this book, if you were able to see that it had to be the hand of God that kept me from dying physically and spiritually and would like to have Him as your personal savior, I invite you to say this prayer:

Lord, forgive me of my sin. Come into my heart and change me from the inside out. Lord, I believe that you sent your son to die for me and he will come back one day and take us to Heaven to spend eternity with you.
In Jesus' name, amen.

CONGRATULATIONS! If you said that simple prayer, I believe you are saved. Reach out to your local church or contact me at **pdulin73@gmail.com** so we can discuss the next step to becoming exactly who God has created you to be.

Promises

I want to leave you with a few scriptures that I referred to very often during my wilderness experience. I pray that you find one or two, three or four to be helpful, uplifting and encouraging.

Promises Of

Love – Psalm 89:38; Isiah 54:10; Jeremiah 31:3-4; Matthew 10:30-21; John 3:16; 15:9, 13; 1 John 1:9

Forgiveness – 2 Chronicles 7:14; Psalm 103:8-12; Jeremiah 31:34; Luke 15:3-7; Acts 10:43; Ephesians 1:7; 1 John 1:9

Peace – Psalm 29:1; Isaiah 26:3; John 14:27; Romans 5:1-2; Ephesians 2:14; 2 Thessalonians 4:17

Joy – Psalm 16:11; John 15:10-11; 16:22; Romans 16:13; 1 Peter 1:8;

Freedom – Psalm 119:32; 146: 7; John 8:34-36; Romans 6:6, 14, 20-22; 2 Corinthians 3:17; Revelation 1:5

God's Promise When You:

Feel Guilty – 2 Samuel 14:14; Psalm 130:3-4; Romans 8:1-2; 1 Corinthians 6:11; Ephesians 3:12; Hebrews 10:22-23

Feel Dejected – Psalm 130:7; Isaiah 65:24; Matthew 11:28-30; Roman 8:26-27; Hebrews 4:16; James 4:8, 10

Are Depressed – Deuteronomy 31:8; Psalm 34:18; Isiah 49:13-15; Romans 5:5

Are Afraid – Psalm 4:8; 23:4; Isaiah 35:4; Romans 8:37-39; 2 Corinthians 1:10; 2 Timothy 1:7; Hebrews 13:6.

Doubt – Psalm 34:22; John 3:18; 11:25-26; Romans 4:5; 1 John 4:15-1

Perspectives

What to Read When:

Seeking God's Direction – 1 Kings 3:1-14; Proverbs 2:1-6; Romans 12:1-3; Ephesians 5:15-17; Colossians 1:9-14; James 1:5-8

You Are Tempted to Be Bitter – Psalm 38:7-9; Proverbs 16:32; 1 Corinthians 13; Ephesians 4:29-5:2; Hebrew 12:14-15

Your Faith Needs Strengthening – Genesis 15:1-6; Proverbs 3:5-9; Romans 5:1-11: 1 Corinthians 9:24-27; Hebrews 10:19-25, 35-39; 11:1-12:13

You Need to Control Your Tongue – Psalm 39:1; Provers 10:18-20: Matthew 15:1-20: James 3:1-12

You Are Prone to Judge Others – Matthew 7:1-5; 1 Corinthians 4:1-5; James 2:1-13: 4:11-12

You Are Angry – Genesis 4:1-12; Psalm 4:4; Mathew 5:21-22; 18:21-35; Ephesians 4:25-5:2; James 1:19-21

You Desire Revenge – Deuteronomy 32:34-35; Psalm 94:1; Proverbs 25:21-22; Matthew 5:38-42; Romans 12:7-21; 1 Thessalonians 5:12-15; 1 Peter 3:8-14

You Struggle With Addition – Psalm 18:28-36; Proverbs 23:9-35; Romans 6:1-23; 12:1-2; 1 Corinthians 6:12-20; Philippians 3:17-4:1

What the Bible Says About:

Anger – Genesis 4:1; Psalm 4:4, 38:7-9; Proverbs 16:32; Matthew 5:21-26; Ephesians 4:25-5:2; James 1:19-27

Anxiety – Psalm 94:17-19; Ecclesiastes 22-25; Luke 12:22-34; Philippians 4:4-9; Hebrews 13:5-6

Compassion – Psalm 103:8-12; 116:5-6; Micah 6:8; John 11:17-44; 2 Corinthians 1:3-7; 1 John 3:11-24

Faith – Genesis 15:1-6; Psalm 119:65-72; Provers 3:5-6; Matthew 6:25-34; Romans 3:21-5:11; Hebrew 11

Freedom – John 8:31-41; Romans 8:1-17; Galatians 4:21-5:26

Friendship – Proverbs 17:17; 27:6; Ecclesiastes 4:9-12; John 14:23-15:17; Colossians 3:12-17; 1 John 1:1-17

Grace – Psalm 86; 103; Micah 7-18-20; Luke 15:11-31; Romans 5; Ephesians 2

Happiness – Psalm 33; Isaiah 12; 52:7-10; Matthew 5:1-12; John 13:1-17; Philippians 4:4-9

Hope – Psalm 42; 130; Romans 5:1-11; Colossians 1:3-27; 1 Peter 1:3-9

Joy – Isiah 12; 52:7-10; Luke 15; James 1:2-18; 1 Peter 4:12-19

Love – Leviticus 19:18, 34; Deuteronomy 6:1-5; Songs of Songs 1-2; Mark 12:28-34; 1 Corinthians 13; 1 John 4:7-21

Peace – Numbers 6:24-26; Psalm 122; Isaiah 9:2-7; John 14:25-27; Romans 5:1-11; Ephesians 2:14-18; Philippians 4:4-9

Repentance – Deuteronomy 4:30-21: 2 Chronicles 7:14; Ezekiel 18:30-32; Matthew 4:12-17; Luke 18:9-14; Acts 2:38-41

Revenge – Deuteronomy 32:34-35; Psalm 94:1; Proverbs 25:21-22; Matthew 5:38-47; Romans 12:17-21

P.O. Box 453
Powder Springs, Georgia 30127
www.entegritypublishing.com
info@entegritypublishing.com
770.727.6517

www.ingramcontent.com/pod-product-compliance
Lightning Source LLC
Chambersburg PA
CBHW061919130726

47908CB00017B/2556